E.D. HACKETT

A Trip Down Memory Lane

A Novella

First edition

ISBN: 978-1-7374679-7-7

Editing by Granite Editorial
Cover art by Last Page Press-E.D. Hackett

This book was professionally typeset on Reedsy.
Find out more at reedsy.com

*This novella goes out to all the what-ifs that follow us through life...
may you find your happy ever after.*

Chapter One

⸻

S canning my closet, I grabbed the heavy wool sweater that made my neck itch and my armpits sweat. It didn't belong in my Florida home, but my mom bought it for me last Christmas, encouraging me to wear it on cool winter nights. She always supported the little guy and bragged about how she'd found it at a craft fair. It was cheap, but the quality was superior to anything she'd found hanging on the racks of the department stores. She blessed me with this tacky wool sweater and then sneaked out of my apartment to return to New England.

I held it up to my petite frame, contemplating if it should join me on my trip home. Rolling my eyes at my reflection, I shoved it into my duffel bag. It was the only New England-y thing I owned. I ran around my apartment, pulling out last minute items and piling them at my door, before glancing around and spotting the toes of my sneakers sticking out from beneath the edge of the couch — *I better not forget those.*

My mom had always told me to pack enough clothes for any

season, but the Florida sun had spoiled me. Even when the temperature dropped into the thirties, I decorated my summer attire with a winter hat and scarf, knowing the freezing temps were only temporary.

Those wintry days were not today. The calendar may say February, but it was in the low seventies. It might be snowy and cold in Boston, but it was warm and balmy in my little suburb of Tampa. I slid my feet into my flip flops, checked the air conditioner, watered the plants, and triple checked the appliances and lights. Everything was off, so it seemed my apartment would still stand when I returned next week.

Lifting my duffel bag to my shoulder and down again, I contemplated packing more clothes for my trip into the northern tundra. If I didn't, there was always shopping, whether at the mall or in my college roommate, Lanna's, closet.

Living solo for the last ten years, I only had to think of myself, but sudden pangs of nostalgia hit me at the strangest times. I missed college life, and the sister it had given me for close to a decade. When I moved to Florida, the phone calls and texts diminished over time. Our lives had taken different paths and with each passing year, the distance between us increased. Then COVID hit, and I fell into a depression—broke, unemployed, and alone.

Once the masking restrictions lifted and the numbers went down, Lanna came to visit, toting a giant ring on her finger. "Cas, will you be in my wedding?" she had asked.

Feeling like a bundle of nerves mixed with excitement, I had to say yes. After she had left, the weight of my agreement sat on me like a baby elephant. I didn't know anyone, and I hadn't visited my parents in years.

Lanna and I had lived together during college from start to

2

finish in Boston. With her help, I learned how to share a kitchen, a bathroom, and a bedroom. Being an only child, and coming from a fairly wealthy family, I'd had a hard time transitioning to dorm life. We became close because we had no choice. During freshman year, our college ran out of housing, so they put us up in a hotel beside campus. Our sophomore year, we moved into a suite with two other girls, and our junior year, Kenmore Square became our neighborhood. We stayed there until graduation, and then went our separate ways.

I didn't miss Boston at all. The broken buildings, dirty streets, and nonstop noise nearly killed me. Literally. One night, while walking home from the Italian restaurant I worked at, I had almost got hit by a cab.

The driver had laid on his horn, and slammed on the brakes, but the car's nose nearly touched my shins before it stopped. I remembered feeling glued to the spot, like I had grown up from the pavement, my body an immobile tree trunk and my arms flailing wildly like branches in a storm. The driver had jumped out of his car, screaming with wide eyes and a twisted face, and I had sprinted down the dirty street all the way to my apartment. My heart pumped in my ears and sweat pooled under my coat. I had nearly died. Ever since that incident, I knew I had to get out of there for good.

As soon as I graduated, I got a job somewhere warm and less congested. Florida, the vacation destination, seemed like the perfect place to start over. I needed to be in a place that would allow me to daydream without risking my life. Lanna got a boyfriend, and while we never quite lost touch, we weren't as close as we used to be. She had needed me during COVID and I wasn't in the right headspace to be there for her.

I stared into the mirror, wondering where the fun girl from

2008 went. My spunky, platinum hair had turned black, my svelte body softened, and my immaculate complexion became dry and leathery from the sun. Smearing face cream over my cheeks one last time, I hoped for the best. Maybe the dry, cold air would do me some good.

I grabbed the bag next to the door and raced out of my apartment. For me, five minutes late meant on time, but that's not how the airlines worked. Rushing through the drive, I weaved in and out of traffic, feeling the back of my neck prickle as the roads got busier and busier. An accident up ahead had caused a slowdown, and my heart raced; my lips pursed, and my eyes checked the clock, reminding me I still had plenty of time.

"What in the world is going on?" I wondered aloud, while pulling up my traffic app. This was not good. A red diamond glared at me from the digital route on my GPS, and I clicked on it. "Accident. Right lane closed. Reported 9:43." I held my breath and looked at the image again. It was a short distance before the accident cleared.

I leaned forward and searched for any sign of progress. In the distance, lights flashed, and I let out a sharp sigh of relief. *Lanna will kill me if I miss my flight.*

Her wedding was next weekend, and despite our rocky past, I wouldn't miss it for the world. She was the one who nursed me after too many drinks, listened to me cry when my boyfriends broke up with me, and motivated me to be and do better. It was a shame we had lost touch over the years, but this year was as good as any to reconnect and strengthen our friendship.

My car crept forward, eventually breaking fifteen miles per hour, and I passed the place where the accident had been. All the cars had already been towed, and they left behind a wake of shattered glass and plastic. Every time I passed an accident, I said a brief prayer for their safety, so I mumbled under my breath and weaved around a crushed mirror. The sweat pouring out of my hands slowed as I cleared the last of the debris, and I wiped my palm on my legs. I was going to make it.

As I raced to security, I triple checked my belongings. Wallet, keys, carry-on. I didn't pack a suitcase because I didn't want to spend the extra money, plus I had shipped all the wedding stuff to my parents' apartment the week before. I had hoisted the extra-large box, filled with my bridesmaid dress, shoes, rehearsal dinner dress, and wedding gift onto the post office counter. It barely fit, and probably cost just as much as it would to check a bag, but having one less thing to manage at the airport made the postage worth it.

I settled into a seat at the gate and scrolled through my phone. Lanna's Instagram page popped up, and I scanned through photos of her and her fiancé over the past year. I spied pictures of them standing beside a snowman, wearing Halloween costumes, apple picking, swimming at the ocean, and eating random food. She didn't look a day over twenty-five, yet I knew the truth. We were in our thirties, and the decade of fun was over. At least for me.

I analyzed her fiancé, admiring his deep brown eyes, distinguished nose, and accentuated cheekbones. In some photos, he slicked back his GQ hair, while in others it was spiky, and cut close to his head. Without even meeting him, I knew he was a fashionista, just like Lanna. I hoped I fit in with the wedding party. Clothing styles never mattered to me, and now that I lived in Florida, clothes were optional most days.

The surrounding seats had filled with 9 to 5-ers, moms with

toddlers, and sleep-deprived families. I pulled my bag closer between my feet and smiled at a boy, around the age of two, toddling by. He wore a pair of shorts, appropriate for the seventy-three-degree day, as well as a string attached to two mittens hanging over his shoulders. He was ready for New England winters, and I couldn't help but smile. My smile dropped as my sneakers flashed behind my eyes. They still sat snug between the door and the couch in my apartment. I looked at my pink-coated toenails, peeking out of my thin flip-flops. Unlike that little boy, I wasn't prepared for New England weather. New shoes would be my first purchase, I decided.

A woman who appeared to be in her mid-twenties sat beside me listening to something—music, a podcast, or maybe an audiobook—and flipped through a magazine. I looked out of the corner of my eye and saw the candid shots of celebrities walking the streets or out on vacation.

When she finished scanning the last page and closed the magazine, she asked, "Do you want this? I hate carrying around extra stuff." The magazine cover glistened under the overhead lights, and I couldn't wait to dive into the lives of the rich and famous.

I gave her a warm smile. "You sure?"

"Yeah, once I look through it, I have no need for it."

"You know, I never would have expected someone of your age to read paper magazines. I thought your preferred gossip would be through social media." I caught my gaffe and tried again. "I mean, not you personally. I don't even know you, but other kids your age." A blush crept up my cheeks, and I spoke again to take the attention away from my face. "I mean, I don't know for sure, but you definitely look younger than me."

The woman's eyes returned to her bag as she dug out a candy

bar. "I'm twenty-seven. My name is Jewel. Do you want some?"

"No thanks. I'm Cassidy, and I'm thirty-three."

"What brings you to Boston?" She shoved the candy away and instead popped a piece of gum into her mouth. "You want some?"

"No thanks." Grateful to have someone to talk to, I settled back in my seat.

The movies always portrayed airport travelers as friendly and extroverted, whether it was complimenting clothes or hair, sharing magazines and books, or saving seats. Flying solo, I was happy for the distraction. "My roommate from college is getting married next weekend, and I'm in the wedding."

"Oh cool. I'm going home to see my parents. They moved up there a few months ago, and I haven't been yet. Why they'd move from Florida to Massachusetts is beyond me." Dimples appeared in her cheeks, making her appear playful and kind.

"I went to college up there. I actually grew up in Rhode Island. After I graduated with a culinary arts degree, I thought I'd come down here and make a living at a place people visited for vacation. You know, a place people were fortunate enough to have money to spend."

"Oh, nice," Jewel said. "What restaurant do you work at?"

"Actually, I manage the restaurant at the Waterfront Hotel. It's been great. Its sister hotels are all over the country, which is convenient when you travel a lot. I haven't traveled much since COVID, though."

"Me either. I guess there are perks to every job. Being able to stay somewhere for free or cheap is always a bonus."

I returned to Jewel's magazine, opened on my lap, and commented on the fashion. I had never been one to gussy myself up for a date or buy the latest make-up or clothing trends, and it showed in my overstuffed carry-on.

"What time do we board again?" Jewel leaned across me to get a better look at the screen on the other side of the gate.

I shifted to get a better look and also get more room. "Um, I think we board around one-thirty." Glancing at my watch, I saw we had twenty minutes.

When one-thirty came and went, a jumbled announcement came over the intercom. I wasn't really listening, and barely made out any words. People around me rose, and indistinct chatter filled the gate.

"Let me see what's going on," Jewel said, and I recognized the confusion in her creased forehead. She returned a moment later with her hands shoved in her pockets, dragging her feet across the carpeted floor. "Hey Cassidy?"

"Yeah?" I didn't look up from the article about Meg Miller's journey out of addiction and into sobriety.

"They canceled the flight."

My head shot up, and my eyebrows furrowed. "What? But why?" The magazine fell to the floor, and I jammed it in my bag.

"I don't know. Let me see."

By this time, a large crowd had formed around the customer service desk and Jewel's slight frame disappeared amongst the crowd. I should have gone up with her, but in the past, sudden noises, constant movement, and bright lights caused my body and brain to go haywire, so instead I hung back, waiting impatiently.

My bag buzzed, so I pulled my phone out of my purse and saw a notification on the screen.

Snowstorm. Two feet between tonight and Wednesday, Dad wrote.

Flight's canceled, I texted to Mom, Dad, and Lanna.

It's freezing rain right now, Mom replied.

Oh no! Try to get up here as soon as you can. Don't worry if you have to miss things. I'll catch you up when you get here, Lanna commented.

A small pit fell to the base of my stomach where it fizzled, turning my stomach sour. The sour taste filled my mouth, and I struggled to swallow. *I have to get home in time for her wedding.*

I pulled up the weather app and searched for Providence and Boston. Checking the future cast, I saw a wave of blue roll through the eastern half of the United States. Shades of white, light blue, and navy decorated the screen as the cloud of nastiness overtook the map. *How did I not know this?* It seemed absurd that a major snowstorm was approaching, and I hadn't thought to check the weather. I would have gotten an earlier flight if I had known.

Jewel trudged back to our seats and plopped beside me. "Flight's canceled, along with most of the flights north of DC. They said we can't rebook until tomorrow. What are you going to do?"

I stared ahead, not focusing on anything but the dizzying colors flashing in and out of my vision. "I don't know. I have to get home. My best friend is getting married." My fingers shot to my mouth, and I nibbled on my cuticles.

"Want to drive?"

"My car won't make it. My tires only work on hot pavement, not in two feet of snow."

Jewel gazed ahead, thinking. "What if we rented a car?"

"Who. Us?" My pointer finger went from me to her and she nodded.

"Why not? You need to get home, and so do I. We can split

the cost of the rental. We'll make it up there in two days, once the storm ends."

Shaking my head, I couldn't quite process her words. "But we'll be driving through the storm."

"Think about it. It's not snowing down here. We'll make it up to DC by tomorrow. By then the snow has already moved through New York. We'll stop in DC to give some more time and then make the last eight hours riding the tail of the storm. It'll be fine. And if it's not, we'll stop. We can easily grab a cheap flight out of Philly to Boston if we can't drive any further."

The calendar flipped through my mind, and I considered the craziness of Jewel's plan. I didn't even know her, yet we both had to get up north. Lanna had said I could miss whatever events she had planned this week, but I still had to be there by the weekend. "Um, sure." I wasn't sure, but what other option did I have? Canceling? I don't cancel. *I am reliable and dependable and will do anything for my friends—even drive cross-country up the East coast with a stranger.*

Jewel hopped up from her seat, grabbed her bag, and walked toward the people mover. I quickly followed.

"Do you have any luggage?" I asked from behind.

"No, do you?"

"No." The sky outside was bright blue with white cumulus clouds. It didn't look like snow.

"Great, let's grab a car."

While standing in line for the car rental, I noticed we weren't the only ones with this hare-brained idea. "I hope they have enough cars for all of us." It wasn't just us, but all the passengers from the airlines heading north stood in the lobby.

"One compact car with snow tires and GPS, please." I gave the woman my license. She completed all the documentation and handed me a set of keys.

"It's the last compact car we have, but I promise it has snow tires."

Jewel and I walked outside, following the instructions the woman gave us. At the farthest corner of the parking lot, a bright red MINI-Cooper glistened in the Florida sun. I clicked the lock button and the tiny car blinked and beeped.

"What is this?" I asked. "We can't drive this through snow."

"It's so cute! I can't wait to ride in it." Jewel leaped in the front passenger seat and touched all the knobs and buttons. "Hey Cassidy, can you drive a stick?"

Peeking through the window, I saw the black leather knob with the shifting placement engraved on top. "Oh, no. I should have told her I don't drive manual, but I assumed it wouldn't be an issue! Why do they carry manuals? This is the United States. No one drives these anymore."

Jewel climbed out of the car and readjusted her bag. "I can't either. We either jerk our way out of the parking lot, or we get another."

We marched into the building and the line had diminished, but the crowd cluttering the space in front of the counter grew. "This doesn't look good," I said.

A single man standing in front of us said, "Yeah, they just announced they're out of cars." The cadence of his voice brought me back to high school, but I couldn't place it. He wore an Indy 500 baseball hat, casting a dark shadow over his eyes.

"Are you serious?" I asked. I looked at Jewel. "What are we going to do?"

She stood on her tip-toes and shielded her eyes. "Let's just talk to them and see what they say."

"Are you in line?" I asked the man in front.

He turned back to us. "Uh, no, I already went up there. I'm trying to figure out—hey, wait a minute—Cassidy?" A huge grin spread across his face. "Cassidy McCarthy?"

My hand cupped my chin, and a smile slid up the left side of my lips. "Uh, yes."

"You look different, but I'll never forget those eyes," he gushed.

I stepped back, trying to place the man. A sense of familiarity and home surrounded me, but nothing came to mind. "Do I know you?"

He removed his hat, and ocean blue eyes stared back at me. "It's Dusty. Dusty Michaels."

Yes, Dusty! "No way!" I threw my arms around his neck and gave him a quick hug. "Jewel, this is Dusty. Dusty and I grew up together. Actually, he was my first boyfriend and the first boy I ever kissed." *Among other things.* "Dusty, this is Jewel. We just met at the airport."

His grin nearly touched his ears and his burning eyes stared into mine. "Well, I'll be damned. How many years has it been? Fifteen?"

Suddenly nervous, I ran my hands through my hair, then wiped them on my pants. "Yeah, about that. What are you doing down here?"

"I'm on business. Heading back to Boston, but obviously not today. I was hoping to get a car, but they're all out."

I couldn't break away from his eyes, and tiny vibrations erupted from my insides.

"No, they're not." Jewel's voice poked through our intimate exchange.

Dusty leaned against the wall, and I checked out his slim

figure, muscular arms, and calf tattoo. A familiar feeling wrestled through my heart. He looked good. Pushing my hair out of my face, I hoped I looked good, too.

"What do you mean?" he asked.

"Can you drive a stick?" Jewel's eyes held his.

"Yeah, I race cars for fun." He pointed at his hat.

"Wait, you raced at Indy 500?"

"Uh, no, but I was there. I love racing. I love cars, of course I can drive stick."

"We have a car," Jewel confirmed.

I shook my head at her. "But we can't drive it."

"Right. But he can. Where are you going?"

"I'm trying to get home to Boston," he said.

Jewel grabbed my arm. "Hey, I need to use the bathroom. Come with me for a second?" Her head jerked toward the corner of the room but her eyes stayed locked on mine.

"Sure. Be right back," I said to Dusty.

"Don't go anywhere!" Jewel said.

In the room's crowded corner, she whispered. "Okay, first, the chemistry coming off you two is undeniable. Second, he can drive. Let him drive us."

I looked from Jewel to Dusty and back to Jewel again. "Yeah?"

"Yeah, why not? You need to get home, right? There aren't any other cars."

I contemplated my options before sighing. "Sure."

We walked back to Dusty, and he smiled at me. My breath caught in my chest, unsure if I wanted to spend the next three days driving across the country with my ex-boyfriend.

I swallowed the lump in my throat. "Dusty, we have a car, but it's manual and I can't drive it. Would you like to drive with us? I totally get it if—"

"Sure."

My mouth clamped shut as his deep voice rolled in my head. "Sure?"

"Yeah, let's go."

Jewel grabbed her bag and led the way out of the cramped waiting area. "Follow me."

We got to the car and loaded our bags into a slice of space in the trunk.

A ding echoed from someone's pocket, and we all reached for our phones. "Oh, wait," Jewel said, planting her feet on the ground. Her smile wavered, and she pulled at her bottom lip. "My mom just texted and said that she rebooked my flight for next week." Her weight shifted from one leg to the next, like she was unsure if she should come with us and ignore her mom, or leave us to embark on our journey alone.

She blew air out of her cheeks and retrieved her bag from the trunk. "Guess I won't be going with you after all."

"Wait, you're leaving?" My voice wobbled.

"My new flight is booked, so I guess I'm not coming. Nice to meet you both, and drive safe!"

As we watched her walk away, an urge to run to her and away from Dusty traveled to my toes, but my legs remained frozen to the spot. My mind raced through what had just transpired. *We got this car because it was her idea. We invited Dusty because it was her idea, and now she isn't coming?*

Dusty leaned against the door, his shoulders higher than the roof. "So..."

"So." My heart fluttered in my chest and I swallowed. "Looks like we're going on a road trip."

Playful memories danced behind his eyes. "Let's go."

"I get shotgun," I said, referencing an old inside joke. Memories from driving around in his beat-up Ford Escort flooded my heart. When I was his girlfriend, I always got to ride in the front, even when he picked me up and his buddies were already in the car.

"Just like old times? That means you're navigating."

"And I get music privileges," I confirmed.

As we pulled out of the parking lot, I texted my mom, dad, and Lanna. **Driving up. I should be home sometime on Wednesday. Love you!**

A barrage of heart and kiss emojis filled the screen, and I grinned at the thought of the adventure that was just beginning.

Chapter Two

⊷⊶✦⊷⊶

As soon as we turned onto the highway, a lull settled around me, like the air in my lungs had a slow leak. Everything had happened so quickly in the parking lot with Jewel. Maybe it was more than just a random occurrence. It was as if she had concocted a plan that forced me on an unexpected path, and now here I was, with my ex-boyfriend, in a car for several days. It seemed strange how everything had lined up, but I would never question the Universe.

"So," Dusty said, "How've you been? It's been, what—since our freshman year of college?"

It looked like we were having this conversation, which was about fifteen years overdue. I slouched down in my seat and looked out the window. "Yeah. That was a lifetime ago." I wasn't ready to talk about our break-up. That year, I had made so many mistakes, and I wasn't sure if closure naturally came with time or if discussing the past would slice open the wound again.

I felt Dusty's eyes on me and, when I didn't continue, he filled the space. "So, tell me about you. How'd you end up in Florida? How was college?"

It was an innocent question, but I felt like a jerk. My cheeks burned at the memories I had buried over a decade before. He'd been my first boyfriend. My first everything, really, and I dumped him from my life like a gallon of spoiled milk. I was too young and naïve to fully understand my actions and words toward him, and he deserved a conversation. He had always been my constant, so when I treated him like he was nothing, I should have expected things to implode. "Uh, well, after I graduated, I had this powerful pull to restart my life somewhere else. I mean, I had this degree that I could take anywhere."

"Did you graduate with culinary? You always could turn Ramen noodles into a gourmet meal."

I shifted my body, my muscles molding into the cloth seats, rolling the tension out of my shoulders. "Yeah, I found a job on the beach at a restaurant, and I worked my way through the system. I'm now the manager of a restaurant on the waterfront. It's in a hotel, but we get a lot of local traffic."

He smiled at me and I felt a tug in my heart when his full lips loosely closed. Images of seventeen-year-old me kissing eighteen-year-old him were pictures I had once treasured and then packed away for safekeeping. They fell out of the photo album in my head and scattered at my feet. "I knew you'd do it," he whispered.

My throat thickened, and I cleared it to breathe. "What about you?" I took a sip from my water bottle while waiting for his response. The cold liquid splashed down my throat, turning my parched mouth into an icy river.

"I graduated with my MBA."

My eyebrows shot up. "Wow, good for you. That must have been a tough program to get through."

"Yeah, thanks. I started a tech company. It's a little start up, about five years old."

I could tell he wanted to share more, but didn't want to overshare. I had always loved that about him.

"Wow, that's amazing, Dusty." My hand touched his knee, and I gave a shy smile. His torso stiffened, and I recognized the old patterns I had fallen into. I had somehow stepped over the line, so I pulled my hand away and placed it in my lap. I wanted to look at him, but the air in the car had become stiff and stuffy. To occupy my hands, I readjusted the vents until my long hair flapped in the breeze.

"Thanks. Yeah, it's been quite the journey," he said.

"What brought you down to Florida?"

"Work. We're working with a company whose headquarters are down here. I can't say who." He winked a blue eye at me. "It's a secret, because, you know, security."

His ease put me at ease. I wasn't ready to talk about us, and I didn't imagine he was either. Instead, we settled into a safe conversation about the weather and the looming storm. Our sunny skies had transitioned to murky gray, and it seemed we were chasing the storm north.

"What's your plan?" I asked.

"About what?"

I could have been asking about the next thirty years or the next five minutes. Either way, he appeared unfazed, like we were two friends or lovers going on a vacation. "How far are we going, Cap? You're steering this ship. I'm just a stowaway."

He lowered his voice to a throaty growl. "Well, Cas, we drive north to Richmond."

At the sound of my childhood nickname, my stomach somersaulted. "Is that your captain's voice?"

"Isn't that what they sound like? All deep and proper?" His eyes flashed with mischief.

At that moment, I missed him. His humor and his ability to laugh at himself were qualities I had fallen in love with.

Dusty continued in his regular voice. "If we can get that far before the car veers off the road into a massive snowbank, we'll be right on track to get home by Thursday."

"Okay, Cap, and when do we plan on stopping tonight?" The GPS indicated we would arrive in Boston on Thursday morning with no stops.

"You know, math isn't my forte." His gravelly voice brought me back to the high school plays we both took part in. He was handsome, even then, and until that first cast party, he had never looked twice at me.

"Maybe after midnight?" he continued. "I have insomnia, so I'll be fine, but if you feel like the weather is too scary or I get too tired, we'll stop sooner."

My brain immediately went to Lanna's schedule. I had told her I'd be there to help with any last-minute fires, but the only thing I had to attend was the wedding rehearsal on Friday, and the wedding on Saturday. Even if we stopped for the night…two nights…we'd still get there in time. "You know, I'd rather be safe than sorry. I have to be back by Friday, but it's only Tuesday, right? We got plenty of time."

"Plenty of time," he assured.

By the time we hit South Carolina, the full moon in the black sky lit up the empty freeway.

"How are you doing?" I asked. The clock was nearing midnight and I could see his eyes fluttering as the weight of his lids threatened to close.

"Eh, tired." He cranked up the air conditioning and the vented air swept back the cocoa colored tendrils at the nape of his neck.

"I think we should stop," I said. "Let's get a hotel and we can start fresh tomorrow." I had been texting with Lanna all night, updating her on our progress. I told her I bumped into Dusty at the airport and we were going to drive up together, and she whooped and cheered at how fate had intervened.

"You sure? We haven't caught up to the storm yet."

"Uh, yeah. I'd rather we hit the snow when we're awake and alert. I could really go for a warm, comfy bed." I pulled up my phone and scrolled for a nearby hotel. Like a light bulb going off in my head, I grabbed his arm, and tiny sparks zapped through me. "I have an employee discount. Let me see if there is a hotel nearby that I have access to."

As the car moved up the highway, we passed signs for lodging, food, and gas, and at every exit, Dusty asked, "This one?"

"No, no. We'll get off at the next one. There's a boutique hotel a half a mile away, and it falls under the Morrison Hotel chain. All I have to do is show them my ID and we'll get a fifty percent discount. Why didn't I think of this sooner?"

The car coasted off the highway and onto a main strip in some random town in South Carolina. The hotel entrance lit up, and we drove around the building, looking for a spot.

"Wow. It looks full," Dusty said.

"It's a boutique hotel. They usually have less rooms available."

"It looks like an old apartment building." His voice revealed disappointment, and I couldn't help but wonder if this was the four-star hotel I had grown to expect from Morrison.

"Yeah, actually, it was a candle factory back in the 1800s. I think the website said it only has sixty rooms total."

The MINI-Cooper stuttered and stopped, and I stretched my wobbly legs. The temperature had certainly cooled since we left Florida, but the refreshing air alerted my senses and mind. Maybe it was knowing I'd be asleep in an hour. Whatever it was, I was happy to be here.

I pulled out my carry-on from the trunk and swung my purse over my shoulder. "Let's go."

Dusty reached across me to grab his bag and I smelled a hint of musk. He smelled the same as senior year, and a rush of memories cascaded upon me. We had been in the car for over eight hours, and somehow, we had skated around the topic of relationships. I wasn't sure I wanted to know where the last fifteen years had brought him.

I followed him into the hotel and dug through my purse for my wallet. Hidden behind my license, I found my ID card and showed it to the man at the concierge desk. "Hi, we need two rooms, please, for tonight. Here is my ID. I work at The Waterfront in Tampa." I gave him my brightest smile, but he didn't reciprocate. He dragged my card across the table and his eyes moved from the card to the computer.

"You know there is a conference in town," he said. I looked into his dead-pan eyes, noticing the dark purple rings below.

"No, I-uh-I didn't."

"Yeah, thirty thousand people are here for the bridal expo at the convention center. All the hotels within the area are booked. Let me see if we have anything." He leaned closer to the computer and squinted.

I glanced back at Dusty. "We might be crashing in the car," I whispered with a grin. I was only half-joking, because there was no way we could continue driving. Imagining his lanky body stretched out in the MINI-Cooper, I saw his knee bump the shifter and the car roll down a hill into the hotel.

"You need two rooms?" The man's eyes darted from left to right as he scanned the computer for a room.

"If possible."

"We'll take one," Dusty said. "Whatever you have." He grabbed my waist and pulled me close, making it seem like we were a couple. Familiarity from feeling his body against my own had been dormant for so many years, and it slowly sneaked its head out of the dark corners of my heart.

"I do have one room. Now, you understand our hotel has been under renovation for about four months. We tend not to rent this room because we haven't renovated it yet. Since you technically aren't even staying a full stay, and you work for the company, I can offer it, if you're comfortable staying there."

I knew hotels renovated in spurts, but I had never heard of a hotel not renting a room because it hadn't been renovated yet. "Um, that's fine with me. Dusty?"

"Sure." He yawned for effect, and I elbowed him in the ribs.

"That'll be $59," the man said.

My eyes bulged at the price. In what decade were brand name hotels $59?

"It needs quite a bit of renovation. I gave you a seventy percent discount off regular room price," he explained.

After I handed over my card, he handed us an actual door key, not the usual keycard I expected. "Go to the top floor. Take a right and it's the last door on the left."

Too tired to care about the status of the room, I followed Dusty to the elevator.

"That was weird," I said.

"It's only eight hours. As long as there is a bed, I think we'll be fine."

We walked into the room, and my mouth dropped to the grimy floor. There was no way I was staying here.

Chapter Three

"Look at this room," I said. Dusty's eyes scanned from one corner to the next, looking for a clean, safe place to put down his bag.

Brown stains came into view on the tan rug as I walked further into the room and a general scent of dog swam up my nose.

A scowl pulled at Dusty's lips. "What's the story with this hotel again?"

"An old candle factory turned into apartments, and then purchased by the hotel chain. I bet this was someone's studio." Along the far wall stood three cabinets with two burners built in the counter. Beside that was a sink and a mini-fridge. The full-sized bed had a newer mattress, but someone had stripped it of sheets and blankets.

"Where are we supposed to sleep?" Dusty asked, still gripping his luggage.

I picked up the phone to call the front desk, but the phone was dead. "This is ridiculous." The bathroom appeared clean, but rusty water emptied from the faucet for the first minute. "Yeah, this is a hard pass."

I pulled open the door and Dusty called, "Where are you going?"

"Downstairs. We're not staying here."

I stomped to the elevator, and Dusty followed. Feeling responsible for finding this hotel, I needed to fix it. The emptiness of the lobby sent a chill down my back, and the man smiled from behind his computer.

"Well? Was everything to your standards?"

"No, not at all." I slammed the key on the table. "That room does not need renovations; it needs a blowtorch. Your staff hadn't even made the bed. This is unacceptable." My voice rose in volume, but no one else besides Dusty was in the room. I leaned forward, reading his nametag. "Gavin."

Gavin slid the key from the counter and placed it on the hook behind him. "I'm sorry it wasn't to your standards. That is all we have."

"We're not staying there. I'd like a refund." The clock behind him read one-fifteen. Our pleasant ride had turned into a nightmare.

He handed me a refund slip and apologized again. I stormed outside, and Dusty followed.

"Where are we going to sleep?" he asked.

Dropping my bag on the chilly pavement, I said, "Do you have anything warm in your suitcase?"

"Just my coat."

"I hope you don't mind getting close. We're sleeping in the car." I spoke with a finite tone, and Dusty grimaced.

"Cassidy, I won't fit in there!"

"You will. We'll put the front seat down, and the back seat.

You'll sleep diagonally. Your feet will be under the passenger dash and your head will be in the trunk behind the driver's side. I'm only five feet. I'll curl up in whatever space I can manage. It'll be fine."

"What about our suitcases?"

"Behind the front seats. When we drop the seat back, they'll be under us. It's one night, Dusty. We have to at least try to get some sleep."

With reluctance, he obliged, and pulled out his sweatshirt to use as a pillow. Our carry-on bags slid under the seats before he climbed into the convoluted bed I had created. The car itself was about as wide as a queen-sized mattress but, with the stick shift in the middle, it was more like a twin.

"You get comfy first," I said.

Dusty lay as instructed, and I climbed through the passenger door and snuggled up to his chest. I listened to his heartbeat against my ear and laughed at the absurdity. "Never in a million years did I expect to see you again." I draped his jacket and my wool sweater over our bodies. "And here we are, sharing a MINI-Cooper as a bed."

He readjusted his arm and slid it under my neck. I leaned on my side, using his arm as a pillow. "Please keep me warm," I said.

He pulled me tighter, and I breathed in the scent of his deodorant.

"I know it's late, but I have to ask. Are you dating anyone?" His question caused my stomach to flip, and I became hyper-aware of his chest rising and falling.

"No. You?"

"Not currently. It's complicated."

I didn't want to ask anymore, so instead I settled into the

crook of his arm and stared at the ceiling.

We lay like that until sunrise. I had spent most of the night feeling his body against mine, paying attention to my buried emotions digging themselves out of their graves. My brain ran through the sequence of events from my previous life. Our first date to our first everything, how happy I was, and then prom, and how everything fell apart once college started. I had hung on to him, refusing to acknowledge my feelings, and afraid of disappointing the people who loved me. I was a fool to go to college to be near him, but there had been so much pressure to be the perfect couple. Instead of it appearing desperate, I had considered going to college in the same town romantic. And then the concert, and then the break-up. I was so naïve back then...that person was long gone. I wondered if the Dusty I knew then had also morphed into someone else.

Dusty's stiff movement woke me from my light slumber. My shoulders ached from lying on my side, and my mouth was as dry as a sheet of sandpaper. I couldn't breathe under these close quarters and I opened the car door to get some fresh air.

Digging through my bag, I found an almost empty bottle of water and guzzled it. Confident that I had dampened my terrible breath enough to not be noticeable, I stuck my head back in the car. "Morning, sunshine."

Dusty stretched and his hands hit the roof. "Ouch." He opened the door and rolled his top half out of the passenger side door. "Hey, can you help me? I'm going to fall."

I raced around the car and scooped my arms under his armpits, supporting his body from hitting the ground. "Damn, you're heavy," I said.

"Six feet of goodness."

We looked ridiculous and I couldn't help but laugh. I dragged him out of the car like a dead body and we both ended up on the pavement.

"I can't get up," he moaned, rolling onto all fours.

Delirious from not sleeping, I felt drunk. "Here, let me help you." I used the frame of the car to pull myself up and grabbed his hands. With extra oomph, we leaned against the car. "I say we go into the hotel, use the bathroom and brush our teeth, grab coffee, and hit the road."

"What if he's still there?" Dusty asked.

"Who, Gavin?" I pulled out my toothbrush. "Where's your toothbrush?"

"I got it," Dusty said, rummaging through his bag. "Will he kick us out?"

"No, he'll be gone by now. It's after seven." I grabbed his hand and pulled him toward the hotel entrance.

Just as predicted, Gavin had left, and a woman smiled as we walked by. After using the bathroom, we grabbed a coffee and bagel on our way out. The weather had shifted to blue skies, and I wondered how different life in Massachusetts was at that moment.

On the road again. How's the weather?

Lanna replied with a snowflake emoji. **Coming down hard, but it should be over sometime tomorrow morning. Where are you?**

South Carolina. We'll go as far north as we can. Love you and sorry I'm missing all the festivities. I added a celebration emoji, followed by a hugging emoji, followed by a bride and groom emoji.

Safe travels.

The coffee was stronger than I had expected and I swallowed the black liquid and then grunted. "This stuff'll put hair on your chest."

Dusty put the car in reverse, and we veered onto the highway. "Time to get a move on."

I nursed my coffee until we got to Virginia. The blue skies had turned to gray and raindrops splattered our windshield. "Here we go," I said, bracing myself for the storm.

Chapter Four

⌒⌒⌒⌒⌒

"Hey Dusty? Are you getting hungry?" Not only was my stomach growling, but I was bored. Over the last few hours, the rain had fallen at various intervals, and although it wasn't nighttime yet, it looked and felt like midnight. Our total time in the car skirted around fifteen hours, and we'd seemed to run out of conversation around hour seven.

"Yeah. We'll stop at the next rest area."

I flipped through the radio and settled on pop music. When we were dating, Dusty hated this music. I'd dance around the kitchen singing into a slotted spoon, and he'd stand at the fridge bellowing "LA-LA-LA-LA-LA," over me.

Giggling at the memory, I turned the music up and sang with Gina Fellows. "This is the dance. We gotta dance. Dancing until the sun comes up."

Dusty's deep, exaggerated voice cut through mine. "Touch my body. Yeah, my body. Love me like it's your last dance."

I turned the music off and stared, my mouth agape. "What was that?" I shifted my body to fully face him. His eyes stayed on the road and I took a moment to admire the slope of his nose. He had a prominent nose that never got in the way when we kissed. Picturing his lips on mine, I felt heat rise from my middle to my neck.

"What? I like music."

I fanned myself. "Wow, that was rather sexy. Where was that man fifteen years ago?"

He shrugged and shot me a playful grin. "I learned that it's best to love the music your girlfriend loves."

"That's not why we broke up, you know." My smile and voice dropped.

"Well...maybe if I agreed to go with you to Dina May's concert, things would have turned out differently."

"Dina May? How do you even remember her? She was a one-hit wonder that never put out another album."

"Yeah, well, when your girlfriend breaks up with you, you pay attention to the details."

I uncrossed my ankles and pressed my back against the seat. I guess we were going there. *It was so long ago, he couldn't possibly hold that against me, could he? No, he wouldn't.* "Yeah, about that. I'm sorry. And for the record, I never broke up with you."

Dusty flipped his hand toward me. "Um, you did. If I recall, you avoided me like the plague. I eventually stopped chasing you, and you never once reached out to me." His voice softened and his hand waved toward me. "It happened a long time ago. I believe everything happens for a reason, and I've learned a lot about love and relationships from you."

I didn't respond because I feared whatever words I spoke would either minimize the experience or minimize his feelings. Instead, I did nothing.

"Don't worry." His smile warmed my guilt. "I still love you."

I felt a jolt travel through me, like a ping-pong ball soaring over the net. I wanted to say, "I still love you too," but I knew he said that in jest, to lighten the mood. "Thank you. For forgiving me." I didn't want to talk anymore about what transpired between us during our first year in college. "I'm going to text my parents. Where are we?"

"Richmond." He pulled off the exit ramp, and we coasted into the rest stop. "We need gas, too."

As he pumped gas, I texted my parents, and we went inside to grab food. We ate in silence, and I spent most of the time admiring how he had aged. He no longer looked like the boy from my childhood, but a man who'd weathered some storms over the years. I wanted to dig into his past, and find what defining moments I had missed. What trauma had he endured and where did the scars lie? What was the happiest moment of his life? Did he have any regrets? I wanted to ask, but I couldn't.

Staring into his eyes, I tried to find the layers that covered his fears, his pain, and his joy. He was a mystery to me, probably as I was to him.

"What?" he asked. The skin around his eyes crinkled with his smile.

"Nothing. Just looking at you. I've missed you."

His tone shifted, and he stirred his drink with his straw. "The person you miss isn't me anymore."

I let his words marinate in my head for a moment, soaking into all the hidden crevices that housed my less than stellar moments. "That's good, because the person you knew isn't me, either. It's like we're two strangers meeting for the first time."

"Oh, yeah?"

"Yeah. I'm the same in my core, but life has changed me over the years." It was the closest I had come to an apology. I owed it to him to tell him how sorry I was, and how that first year of college, I cried myself to sleep most nights, not just because my best friend was gone, but because I didn't trust myself or who I was becoming. I hated myself for giving up on us so quickly. "I think both of us needed to change."

He pressed his lips together and gazed out the window. "You ready to go?" he asked and threw his trash in the nearest can.

"Ready as I'll ever be."

When we hit Pennsylvania, we not only hit traffic, but we hit snow. And not just snow, but sheets of it. "Oh, shit," Dusty said.

He downshifted, and the car lurched forward. "Did you do that on purpose?" I gripped the handrail with one hand, and the seat cushion with the other. I couldn't remember the last time I drove through snow.

"Yeah. Just trying to get more traction. I can't really see the brake lights in front or the lines on the road. Maybe we should stop."

Not only was the weather bad, making it difficult to see, but we were also driving through an unfamiliar city. This was my worst nightmare and my body didn't betray me. I struggled to breathe, so I sucked in as much air as possible, forgetting to exhale. A cold sweat broke out on my skin and goose pimples erupted on my arms.

Feeling out of control, my left knee jumped up and down in rapid succession. Lightheaded, I threw my head back and breathed in and out, the way my therapist had taught me throughout my senior year of college.

"Hey, you okay?"

I stared at the ceiling of the tiny car. "Uh-huh. Yeah." Organizing my thoughts and planning my words took too much effort, so I barely managed short and concise. The walls of the tiny car engulfed me as the air inside diminished. "Yeah. Let's stop."

I couldn't look out the window; the visual chaos messing with my head. Irrational thoughts barraged my mind, swirling like a mini twister. Despite knowing the likelihood of a serious accident was small, my brain could only process the possibility of dying in a car crash. *It happens all the time. As luck would have it, I would die beside Dusty.* I closed my eyes to block out any movement in my periphery. *Oh, the irony.*

"You okay?" he asked again.

"We need to stop." I exhaled, held my breath for a few seconds, and then inhaled for six. My chest hurt and my icy body rebounded with flames.

"I'm trying." I heard the panic in Dusty's voice, triggering another round of catastrophic events to unfold in my mind.

I didn't open my eyes, but asked, "Is the snow letting up at all?"

"No, it's really bad." After a second of silence, he asked, "Are your eyes closed?"

"Uh-huh."

"Are you having a panic attack?"

"Uh-huh. I don't do snow and driving. We're in a tin can. We're not meant for snow." I tried to swallow and choked on a mouthful of air.

"It's okay. We'll be fine. I live in Boston and drive in this all the time."

"But what about the people who don't?" I squeaked out, my voice monotone and tiny. "What about them?"

He placed his hand on my thigh. This tiny gesture seemed to bring me back to Earth and away from the world of catastrophes. "I got this."

The kindness in his voice reminded me we wouldn't die on his watch. I slowly opened one eye and saw a sea of blinking lights. "What's going on?"

"Accident. We're getting off at the next exit. It's a suicide mission if we keep going."

As my brain recognized the word suicide, my heart raced and my mind fell down the rabbit hole again. "K. Tell me when we get there."

His thumb rubbed up and down my thigh and I focused on the feeling of his fingers on my body. My heart slowed and the ice in my veins melted. I counted to one-hundred with each stroke.

"We're here." The car inched to a stop, and I felt my body melt into the seat. When the engine turned off, I opened my eyes and threw my arms around Dusty, burying my head in the crook of his neck.

"Thank you for getting us here safely," I whispered. Tears that I had been holding back started to flow down my cheeks.

"Jesus, Cassie, are you okay? I didn't know you had so much anxiety."

I pulled away and looked into his eyes. Trust shined back at me. "I don't know if you know this, but the reason I never came home after graduation was because my dad lost his job and my parents ended up filing bankruptcy."

Dusty's eyes circled my face, and he cupped my chin. "I knew they downsized, but didn't know why."

"Yeah, it wasn't something they were proud of. I felt responsible because they were paying my college tuition, and if I had just transferred to a local college, they may have been able to save their house. I was ashamed to face them unless I had proved my education was worth losing everything over. I started having panic attacks my senior year, leading up to finals. The pressure to graduate and get a good job was too much. I took on two part-time jobs, plus my senior requirements, plus job searching."

He stroked my hair, and the feel of his familiar hands comforted me. "I had a mental breakdown." I looked away from him, ashamed of my emotional weakness. Glancing up, I said, "Don't worry. I see a therapist, but the snowstorm triggered something in me. I'm okay now."

He didn't respond, but continued to touch my hair, tucking it behind my ears. Like a faucet, tears erupted, rinsing away my shame.

When I opened my eyes, his upper face filled my vision. His blue eyes, outlined in green, revealed myself reflected in his large pupils. Sad and searching, I couldn't look away.

"You're beautiful, you know."

I pulled away and chuckled. "Beautiful and broken."

He guided my chin with his hand. "No, not broken. You're human, and your strength makes you more beautiful."

I closed my eyes and tilted my head toward him.

Like a magnet, his lips brushed mine and all my insecurities and vulnerabilities washed away in the snow. It happened so fast, I didn't know if I had imagined it. I opened my eyes, and he fiddled with the keys.

"You ready?"

I nodded. Unsure of what just happened, I climbed out of the car, sliding along the icy pavement. Maybe I had imagined it.

Chapter Five

꧂

D usty paid for the motel room, requesting a room with two queen beds. I was grateful we were sharing, as I wasn't ready to be alone. Sometimes feeling someone's presence, even when touching wasn't allowed, comforted me. Still reeling from the kiss in the car, I reminded myself that we were two old friends going on an adventure. Until we talked about what had happened between us, I deserved to be alone. If my parents had taught me anything, it was that the floor could fall out from under you at any moment, so never get too comfortable. Never let security cloud your vision, because it's always temporary. I felt safe with Dusty, despite the many years we'd been apart, but I knew once we got to Boston, we'd be saying goodbye. Again.

I followed him back outside to our room. We were on the second floor overlooking the parking lot. The slick stairs had about two inches of snow, and the loose railing wobbled in my hand as I climbed the rickety staircase.

"This is really slippery," I said over the howl of the wind. My foot slid the width of the plank because my flip-flops were not built for this kind of weather.

"Yeah, watch your step and hold on to the railing."

This motel wasn't nearly as nice as the hotels I usually entertained, but this was the first hotel off the highway. It had a room available, and I couldn't imagine it was any worse than the candle factory.

"Thanks for getting the room."

Dusty let us in and flipped the light. Two beds waited for us, with a white down comforter draped over the edges. I ran and flopped on the bed, kicking off my snowy shoes and climbing under the covers. "I get this bed." Something about being closer to the bathroom wall rather than the wall with windows made me more at ease. "This is nice." I snuggled under the blanket and sighed happily.

Not quite matching my enthusiasm, Dusty pulled down the blankets and inspected the sheets before dropping his bag on the dresser and using the bathroom.

When he emerged, he wore basketball shorts and an oversized t-shirt that said, "PC-Tech," across the front. The shirt sleeves tugged at his biceps, and a small mountain emerged below the hem of his sleeve. He was paler than I remembered, but also stronger. His thighs practically filled out the leg of his shorts, and I couldn't help but smile.

"Nice shirt. Is that your company?"

"Nah, this was from a conference I spoke at. Every guest got a swag bag, and this shirt was one of our gifts." He turned around, and I saw a long list of sponsored companies. "I'm on the back." He sat on the bed and stretched his legs.

"So much better than the car, isn't it?"

Dusty pulled out his phone and nodded at me. "I have to

make a phone call." He excused himself to the bathroom, and I couldn't help but wonder who he was talking to. My battery was nearly dead, so I charged it in the outlet beside the closet. **We're in Pennsylvania right now. Almost home! I'll see you tomorrow,** I texted to my parents and Lanna. I followed it with a car, a snowman, snowflake, a bride, a champagne glass, dancing, and heart emojis. Whoever invented emojis was brilliant. They communicated so much when I couldn't find the words.

I flipped on the television and scrolled through the channels, eventually stopping on the news. I wanted to get home, but also needed a distraction to avoid another panic attack. Now that one had happened, another was sure to come quick.

After watching a segment on a daycare recently shut down, an advertisement for a high school play this weekend, and a segment on the mayoral race, the meteorologist walked across the screen. "Dusty, weather's on!" I called through the motel room.

Her name flashed across the screen and a large map filled the background. "It is now snowing and we've had reports of whiteout conditions across the county. If you look at the map, you'll see the jet stream carrying the precipitation northward through New York, to Boston, and then Portland. So far, approximately five inches have fallen, and another three more are expected before morning. Higher elevations will expect more. Snow clears out around nine a.m. tomorrow and skies will brighten."

"Hey Dusty!" I walked toward the closed bathroom door.

"Yeah?"

"Snow's stopping by tomorrow morning. We should be fine. If it's stopped here, it should stop by the time we get home."

"Okay, cool. I'll be right out."

His voice dropped to a hush and I couldn't make out the words. It sounded serious, so I tiptoed back to the bed and scrolled through the channels.

When Dusty came out of the bathroom, a frown had replaced his smile. His hunched posture and quick movements reminded me of the time he failed Algebra II. I scurried out of the bed and shuffled over to him. "Hey. Are you okay?" I ran my hand up and down his arm and his face paled.

"Yeah, yeah. I'm okay. Just got some bad news from home. I don't really want to talk about it right now."

He pulled away from my touch and lounged on his bed.

The air in the room thickened and the fun, jovial atmosphere from earlier was replaced with confusion. *What news could he have received? And when he said home, did he mean his apartment or did he mean his family? Was it any of my business?* My mind raced like a hamster on a hamster wheel. When I looked over, he had his hands pressed against his face and his eyes fixated on the ceiling. I followed his eye gaze and saw a water stain.

"Do you want any food? There has to be a place nearby that will deliver in the snow." I made my voice as gentle as possible.

"Uh. Yeah. I'll go down and talk to the guy in the lobby. You want pizza?"

I nodded. "That'd be great."

Dusty threw on his sneakers and left the room. "Be right back."

About an hour later, my stomach growled, and I poked through my bag, searching for any misplaced snacks. I came up empty and instead picked up my phone to call Dusty. Scrolling through my contact list, I realized I had never gotten his number. Dread bubbled up inside my belly, as I imagined him laying at the bottom step because maintenance hadn't shoveled. My nerves clashed with hunger, and a booming grumble erupted from my abdomen. *Where was he?*

To pass the time, I checked the door lock and took a shower. If he wasn't out by the time I was done, I'd go to the lobby and find him. The water pressure wasn't great, but the scalding heat poked at all my nerves. I inhaled the steam and let the warmth circulate through my limbs.

I was tired from the trip, and nervous about Lanna's wedding. This week was an opportunity to get to know her fiancé, reconnect, and celebrate their love. Now it looked like I'd be racing in like a tornado, barely able to hear their I Dos. Disappointed was an understatement.

The last time I saw Lanna was when she visited Florida last year. COVID restrictions had just ended, but she still insisted on wearing a mask at all times. I thought she was ridiculous until she told me her grandparents had both died from the virus. Feeling like an asshole for not being there for her, and not knowing the pain she had lived through the previous year, I pulled a mask over my face for the rest of her trip. She needed me and I wasn't there. No wonder we had grown apart.

She'd told me Graham was the reason she'd survived the pain COVID caused. She met him at a bar, and his extravagance had swept her off her feet. While we sat at the pool, she talked about the jewelry, fancy restaurants, and flashy weekends away. It was cute at first, but envy over her luck finding someone ate at me. My jealousy was another reminder that I wasn't the good friend I thought I was. As day one of hearing about Graham turned into day three, and she was leaving on day four, his name made my smile drop and my stomach turn. I reminded myself I was happy for her, and I filed the negative emotions away.

I didn't want to dislike him, but her lust and puppy dog love had ignited feelings that made my skin crawl. I wanted that for myself, and seeing her so in love sparked an ember of jealousy.

I wanted to get to know him, and them as a couple this week, because she deserved happiness. We all did.

After my shower, I slid my bare feet into my purple flip-flops and gingerly descended to the main floor. The snow had accumulated and three people shoveled the walkway below. I found Dusty sitting in the lobby, staring into the parking lot.

"Hey," I said. "How's the hunt for food coming?"

His smile reappeared, and he looked at his watch. "I ordered pizza about an hour ago. They told me they were running late because they only had one driver, but I didn't expect it to be this long."

Sitting beside him, my thigh brushed his, and he shifted a bit away. Ignoring his slight, my eyes fell to my hands, and I turned my body to face him. "I'm starving," I said, pretending I hadn't noticed his rejection.

"Me too."

"Did you ask the guy working if there was any place else?"

Dusty nodded. "Yeah, but I can't drive that clown car in the snow and he said the pizza place is the only place that delivers. Do you want to wait with me?"

Despite his earlier snub, I scooted closer to him and perused his phone from over his shoulder as he scrolled social media.

"Is that your sister?" I asked, as a brunette in a bathing suit on a boat scrolled by.

"Yeah. Rebecca's married now to this guy from Alabama."

"Alabama! I never thought she'd move down south."

Dusty and I looked at a picture of Rebecca and her family. A handsome man wearing designer shades stood beside her. A small child snuggled into his broad chest, and a dog smiled at the camera.

"Aw, they are so cute," I said.

"Yeah, she loves it down there. That's her husband, Dale, and her son, Evan."

"They look happy. I always liked your sister."

"She liked you, too. Do you remember that time you baked her a cake because my parents forgot her birthday?"

"Mmm...you told me how sad she was. She was, what, thirteen? That's a big age."

"Yeah, that was the one and only time they forgot. She's never let them forget how you turned her birthday from the worst day ever to a day she'd always remember with the best cake she's ever had. She looked up to you."

We went on like that, chatting about mutual friends and family. I pulled out my phone and showed pictures of my apartment, my friends, and our old mutual friends. As his body relaxed, the topic of girlfriends nudged me. As each beautiful friend or follower on his feed moved past my eyes, I couldn't help but wonder which one was 'complicated'. He may have mumbled that word earlier, but I had heard it clear as day. Then, with the phone call in the bathroom, maybe 'complicated' didn't mean over.

"Show me your ex-girlfriends."

His finger froze on the screen and he gazed at me with sudden focus. "You sure?" His body crept closer to mine.

"Yeah, totally. I want to know everything."

"Okay. Well, this is Sasha. We dated for about two years."

"Why'd you break up?"

"It wasn't the right time." He didn't expand, and instead

43

moved onto a picture of a woman gazing away from the camera toward a beautiful sunset. "And this is Jo. She lives in Boston."

The shadows created a silhouette embedded against the pink, purple, and orange hues above the horizon.

"How long did you date for?"

"I've known her for about five years."

My eyes widened. He hadn't answered my question, and I clicked my tongue, not wanting to pry. "Wow, long time."

"Yeah, it's complicated." He clicked his home button, and the pictures disappeared.

The word complicated rolled around my head again, and I knew in my gut she was the woman on the phone.

"What about you?" he asked.

"Since college, I've had three relationships. Liam and I dated for about a year, and he just wasn't for me. I was in college, still finding myself, and his lack of direction in life excited me. It was like he made me question the purpose of plans and goals, and I liked it, but after a while it got boring."

A quiet laugh filled the room. "You? Without a plan? I can't believe it. The only reason I got into college was because you gave me that timeline thing, breaking down everything I had to do to apply."

"Yeah, he was a terrible fit, but lots of fun. The second was this man named Taylor. He was older than me, and again, the timing wasn't great. He wanted to get married and have kids, and I had just graduated and moved to Florida. I could barely remember my address. There was no way I was ready to settle down. And the last guy was Tommy. I met him at a club on my twenty-seventh birthday. It was lust at first sight, but there wasn't much substance behind that. When I turned thirty and COVID hit, I decided to fall in love with myself and really get to know me. So, it's been a few years." I felt a tug in my pelvis, surprised that my body was reacting this way. "I mean, I've dated, but nothing serious," I clarified. The last thing I wanted was for Dusty to think I was cob-webby down there. My face went hot and my hands spewed sweat. "Sorry."

A bell beside me jingled and Dusty jumped from the couch and greeted the pizza delivery man at the door. "Finally," he said as the man brushed the snow off his shoulders and hair. "Thank you." Dusty grabbed the pizza boxes and bag of drinks, and pulled a twenty out of his back pocket. "For your inconvenience."

The guy waved and walked out the door. I followed Dusty up to our room and the aroma of cheese and pepperoni taunted me. My stomach growled and I hugged my empty stomach. I grabbed a slice and held it in my bare hands.

"This is amazing," I gushed as a string of hot cheese hung from my lip. "How is it still hot?" I swallowed the slice in five bites, barely feeding the hungry monster in my stomach fast enough. "So good."

I reached for another piece and Dusty pointed at his chin. "You got something."

Suddenly embarrassed for being a pig and a slob, I wiped aimlessly at my face. "Did I get it?"

"Yeah, but right here." He pointed again.

"Good?" I asked.

He approached me with caution and licked the tip of his finger before running it across my chin. "Got it." His finger rested on my face and my heart leaped out of my chest.

"Thank you." I stared into his eyes, unable to look away. Fireworks erupted behind my eyes, and I couldn't help but wonder what it would be like to kiss him. For real this time.

Not just a quick peck, but a deep, intense kiss that knocked my socks off. I wanted to feel him. A lust so strong, my neck leaned toward his, waiting for reciprocation.

Just as his head tilted to the left, my phone rang. Dusty pulled away, and said, "You should get that."

The moment had broken, and I was left with a racing heart, sweaty palms, and a burning desire.

Chapter Six

"Hello?" I gasped, fumbling to put the phone up to my ear as I ran into the bathroom, needing some space to calm my frantic mind.

"Hi Kitty-Kat, it's Mom." I couldn't help but smile, at hearing her childhood nickname for me.

"Hi. How are you?" I turned the faucet on and splashed the cool liquid over my flushed face.

"Good, good, I just wanted to see where you were?"

"Um, at a hotel right now. I think we'll be home tomorrow." My mouth moved and words came out, but my thoughts zapped like a pinball in an old arcade game. Things felt right until they felt wrong. I saw the lust behind his eyes, held hostage by all the unspoken words we both held onto like buried treasure.

I didn't want to dig up the past. He was fine, and so was I, but I owed it to him to at least acknowledge how sorry I was for hurting him. Maybe he had forgotten, but he deserved to know the truth.

Mom's voice rattled in my ear. "Bye Cas. I'll see you soon.

Call me when you get closer."

Hanging up the phone, I readjusted my hair and exited. Second-guessing my interpretation of what almost happened, I shuffled to the bed and bit the inside of my cheek. His back was to me, and I studied the way his hair curled just below his hat, and how his broad shoulders pulled at his t-shirt. He had aged well.

"Sorry about that." My tiny voice barely carried to the television, let alone to him. He didn't turn, and I slowly approached, my heart beat getting louder. I needed to talk to him, but the words froze in the back of my throat, so I tried to swallow them down. "Hi."

His radiant smile painted his face, but I saw the confusion behind his eyes. Knowing he wanted me just as much as I wanted him reminded me that perhaps I was desirable after all. "Hi, again." A flirty air hung onto his words.

Bravery rose through my chest as I sat down. "Can we talk?" I hated those words.

"Oooookay."

"I don't want to bring up old news, but can we talk about us?"

"Oh no," he joked, "are you giving me the it's-not-you-its-me speech?"

I smacked him playfully on his upper arm. "No. I'm talking about that I-hope-I-didn't-hurt-you speech."

His smile dropped. "Oh. You mean back when we were eighteen and you ditched me for that guy you met at that concert? And then never returned my calls?"

The room became still. Even the hands on my watch had stopped ticking. "Yeah, about that."

"I don't really want to talk about it, but since you brought it up, we can't have that talk because you did hurt me."

48

He held my gaze. I wanted to break away, but I knew he deserved my full attention. "I'm sorry," I said.

"You know I loved you."

"I loved you too. I followed you to Boston to be close to you. I thought you were the one."

Looking wounded, he stared at the corner of the room. I reached out to touch him, to show him I still cared, and he jerked his hand away.

"Why'd you have to bring this up?" he asked. "We were having such a nice time. Two old friends stuck in a car together. You know I don't do feelings, Cassie. This is no good for me."

"We need to clear the air!"

"But do we? After tomorrow, I'm never going to see you again. You're doing your thing and I'm doing mine. This is just a coincidence. We were at the same place at the same time and had the same goal. It made sense for us to drive together."

I chuckled. "Well, I needed you for your driving skills."

He didn't chuckle back, but a strained smile slid across his face. "We live on separate sides of the country. Why dig up the past now? You never thought to reach out to me before."

Poking at my cuticles, I contemplated my answer. "But I did. I did call you, and you ignored me. You never picked up."

"Yeah, months later. It was too late. You broke my heart." His eyes narrowed and spittle flung from his mouth. "Maybe I wanted you to try harder. Sooner."

"You know, you're right. We're never going to see each other again, so I'm just going to say it. Seeing you stirred something in me I thought had died a long time ago. And I'm sorry for hurting you. I was young, and stupid, and I thought you were Mr. Reliable. Like I could do anything and you would always be there."

He paced the room, avoiding eye contact. "Like, go on a date with another guy? You didn't want me, and you humiliated me. And then I had to risk bumping into you around the city. It was too much. You tossed me to the side for some random guy. What was his name again?" His eyes searched mine.

"Um, I think Trevor."

His hands soared to his sides. "See? You don't even remember. That's how important I was to you. So important, you can't even remember the name of the guy who replaced me, if only for a moment."

"We were on a break," I said.

"I was your boyfriend."

Throwing my hands up in the air, realizing how wrong this conversation had turned, I said, "Whatever, Dusty. I'm sorry I said anything. But for the record, you told me you needed space. Trevor and I weren't serious." Turning on my heel and trudging to the bed, the weight of the blanket against my head blocked the light. "Good night." It wasn't even eight o'clock yet, but it was this or the bathroom. I slipped my hand out from under the covers and fumbled for my phone.

I can't wait to get home. I texted Lanna. **I hope you're having fun this week getting ready for the big day.** To hide my hurt, I sent her an emoji of someone dancing, a bottle of champagne and a bouquet.

Dusty flipped on the television and turned it down to an inaudible murmur. At least he was respectful enough to let me sleep. I focused on the laugh track from the television and listened to the actors get in and out of random shenanigans. Closing my eyes, I pictured them in my head, focusing on their problems, not mine.

The past forty-eight hours had been a whirlwind.

At some point, Dusty turned off the television and shut off the bedside lamp. I pulled my head out from under the covers and saw him in the shine of the streetlights outside our window.

"What time are we leaving?" My voice carried into the silence and I watched him roll away from my side of his bed. "Dusty? Did you hear me?" Exasperation tainted my words.

"Seven." It was definitive and cold.

"Okay."

A childhood memory of going on vacation with my parents flashed through my head. We drove to Niagara Falls one year, and I was too excited to sleep, especially when we slept at a hotel. Hotels were fancy and fun, and they always had snacks in the lobby. Going swimming was the highlight of the trip, because we didn't have a pool at home, and the indoor pool was the coolest.

My parents always tried to get me to sleep, but I'd talk their ear off in the dead of night. They had learned that if they answered my questions with as few words as possible, I'd eventually shut up. I got the same impression from Dusty.

My body yearned to be next to his, but I wouldn't allow myself to grovel. I had already apologized, and that wasn't enough. After my last relationship, I had vowed to stay single forever. There was no point in having a man. Whatever he could do, I could do better, and I liked my freedom. My neighbors and the restaurant staff had become my family. I had been on a few dates over the past few years, but no one carried that spark that lit my soul on fire.

I missed Dusty and how comfortable I felt around him. He hadn't changed a bit, and if anything, his growth was a turn on. I rubbed the cool space beside me, pretending it was him and we were together in his childhood bedroom. I was so young then, but so was he, and we were perfect for each other.

I missed Lanna too, with her crazy antics. When I walked into our college dorm room freshman year, her small stature carried a buoyancy that kept me afloat after many cry fests. Whether it was men, grades, my parents, or complete overwhelm, she was there for it all. My heart lifted just thinking about her.

My mind shifted to the package I had shipped to my parent's house with the bridesmaid dress, shoes, and gift. Now that I thought about it, my parents hadn't called me to say it came, but I had only sent it out a few days ago, so I still had time. Dread dripped along my insides. *I hope they got it. I'll text them in the morning. Lanna would kill me if I showed up without a dress.*

My brain didn't stop. Being in the same room with Dusty brought up too many memories, and I wasn't tired.

When rough snores filled the room, I grabbed the second pillow and shoved it over my head. I didn't remember him being a snorer, but we did little sleeping those days. I got little sleep that night, too.

* * *

The next morning, my body ached from the lumpy mattress, and my head hurt from dehydration. My sticky mouth tasted like sandpaper, and I wondered how many ounces of salt I had consumed from all the takeout and fast-food restaurants we hit up on the drive.

"Cassie, time to get up." The mattress bounced under Dusty's hands. His gentle pushes turned harder and faster, and I recalled the time we made love on the water bed at his parent's lake house.

"Ugh, I'm up, I'm up." I pulled myself to a sitting position and glanced toward the window. Beautiful white coated the pavement and trees. The comforter and pillows from his bed lay on the floor between our two beds, and I furrowed my brow. "Rough night?"

"Yeah, there's a leak." He pointed at the ceiling, and I saw a tiny drop fall onto the bed below. "I couldn't sleep under it, so I moved to the floor."

A heavy sigh escaped from my chest, and I winced, realizing he chose the floor over sharing a bed with me. All had not been forgiven. "I'm sorry. We'll get you some coffee." I glanced at myself in the mirror across the room and made a face at my disheveled hair and swollen face. "What time is it?"

"Six-ten. It stopped snowing, so I think once we get out of the parking lot, we'll be fine."

I gathered my clothes and disappeared into the bathroom. The hot shower prickled my skin like gunshots and I welcomed the pain. When I got out, my head had cleared and the achiness in my muscles had liquidated.

Scanning the contents of my bag, I pulled out a maxi dress that only an idiot would wear in the middle of winter. Wishful thinking and dreaming of a shopping trip had prevented me from packing smart. I threw it on and pulled my wool sweater over the top. It was good enough.

By the time I got out, Dusty was ready to go. He sat at the small round table beside the window with his suitcase beside him. Entranced with his phone, he didn't notice me.

"Hey, I'm ready whenever you are." My flip-flops provided no comfort from the cold, and I silently scolded myself for the millionth time for not grabbing my sneakers before I left. "Do you have an extra pair of socks?" I asked.

Dusty rummaged through his bag and threw a sock ball at

me.

"Thanks. I need these for the car."

The air temperature had risen slightly since last night, and the wet snowflakes tangoed with ice pellets. Each step down the stairs sounded like a giant coming through the forest. We put our belongings in the trunk, and Dusty settled behind the wheel. I rested my head against the window and tossed his jacket over my legs. "Thanks," I said again. "I never said I was good at packing."

"Or driving," he added, and I stretched my legs along the area under the dash.

"Sure is comfy," I joked.

He pulled out of the parking lot and we fishtailed to the stoplight. I gripped the handrest, praying I didn't have another panic attack.

"We're golden," he said as we veered onto the highway. As we got up to speed, we trailed a snow plow pushing the slushy mess into the breakdown lane. "We'll be home in about six hours."

Home. What a strange term. Since college, I had only visited my parents' apartment a few times. I didn't even come home every year for Christmas because the holidays, although slowest at the restaurant, were also the time when staffing depleted. No one wanted to work at Christmas, so I did. That was the responsible thing to do as a manager. When the restaurant shut down during COVID, and tourism slowed to a snail's pace, I spent my days and nights alone in my apartment, too afraid to leave.

"I haven't been home in about five years," I said.

"You haven't?" I heard the incredulity behind his voice.

"No. I run a restaurant. I can't just leave for weeks at a time."

"But you're taking a week off now. How'd that happen?"

I sighed, not really wanting to get into it. "If you must know, it is February. The holidays are over, so the influx of visitors diminishes."

"Uh huh. Isn't Valentine's Day one of the busiest?"

"We hired a new manager. The first thing I asked when he picked up shifts was if I could take off for Lanna's wedding. She's expecting me, and I couldn't let her down."

"Ah ha. I knew there was another reason. Why don't you come home any other time of the year?"

"Because Florida is crazy from April on. Besides, I like it down there. Seeing my parents in their tiny one-bedroom apartment is a reminder that I cost them their life. I don't want that. I always assumed the best way to say thank you for their sacrifices is to work hard and prove myself. If I'm home visiting, I'm not working hard."

"I see, so it's this weird guilt trip thing you have going on." His lips creased into a thin line, and I could see regret in his eyes, like he wondered if guilt had played into our story.

"It's fine. They visit me at least twice a year. I pay for their airfare. Florida is a much better place than Rhode Island. Trust me. There's more to do, the weather's better, and for them it's a vacation. When I go home, I have to crash on their couch. It's a little awkward, and I don't like it, so I don't do it."

"So five years, huh?"

"Yes, five years since I've gone home, not five years since I've seen them. It'll be fine." I was convincing myself more than convincing him. This visit had been weighing on me since I booked my flight, and I hoped I was strong enough to tuck away all the emotions of responsibility and inferiority.

"Now's as good a time as any to go home."

As the snow turned to rain, and eventually to pockets of

cloudy skies with hints of blue, my anxiety rose. I had pushed myself away from the people who meant something to me in my earlier years, and now I had to face them all in one weekend.

Chapter Seven

When we crossed into Rhode Island from the Connecticut border, I stretched my legs, rolled down my window, and sniffed the icy, salty air. "For some reason, the scent of Florida differs from the scent of Rhode Island."

"It's the cold air. It cleans everything out."

Our little car made it, the engine revving with a high-pitched hum, and the back occasionally fishtailing as we accelerated up the hills. "At least we missed the storm. I'll be happy to get out of this car." My head turned to the left. "No offense."

He waved me off. "Am I taking you to your parents' house?"

My fingernail moved to my mouth, and I nibbled on the dead skin around it. "Um. I can't drive this car and it's in my name, so I think we should drop it off at the rental place. Yeah, we'll return this one. I'll pick up another one, and drive you to your place before heading to my parents. Where do you live again?"

He checked the time. The bright sun sat almost directly above us, and the warm beams brightened my mood. "I'm out near

Framingham. Are you sure? I guess we didn't think of this when we embarked on our trip."

"Yeah, it's fine. Let's go to the airport in Warwick and swap out the cars. Besides, I don't know if I'm ready to see my parents just yet. You'll be doing me a favor."

We still had about a forty-minute ride, and I had a sinking feeling this was our last goodbye. "So," I cleared my throat, "tell me about you. What's going on with your complicated girlfriend?" I wanted to air-quote the word complicated, but knew I'd look childish, so I sat on my hands, like it was no big deal.

"Uh." His nervous eyes moved to mine and then returned to the road again. "We've been on-again-off-again for about six months now. I like her. I do, but we're that couple that loves and fights hard. It's not the healthiest, I know that, but there is something about her that keeps me on my toes."

I smiled, egging him on with my eyes to tell me more. "What's she look like?" It really didn't matter, but it mattered to me. *Was she younger than me? Prettier? Smarter?* I needed to know what I was up against.

"She's petite, with long brown hair and blue eyes."

"What's she like?" I feigned innocent interest, but I was dying to know how his tastes had developed over the years.

"She's one of those people that walks into a room and overpowers everything around her. People can't help but stop and stare because she commands their attention. That was what first drew me to her, but now that I've gotten to know her, I've realized that her need to be the center of attention is draining. For me. I'm constantly needing to take a break from her. We aren't serious, and I know she's dating other men."

A slight gasp escaped from my lips. "And you're cool with

that?" The Dusty I remembered was not okay with me going on a date with another man, no matter how inconsequential it was. I knew that from experience...or maybe I had just assumed that. Maybe it was my guilt that kept me away.

"Not really, but I'm trying to be open to other women, too. I could never be in an open relationship if I'm dating someone I really cared about, but with her...it doesn't bother me. Which makes me think I'm not that into her."

My stomach quivered at his admission.

His eyes glanced toward me and back to the road. "Does that make me a horrible person?"

"No, not at all. It makes you human. It sounds like the sex is great, but the longevity isn't."

I watched a small blush travel up his neck. "Yeah, you could say that."

"Are you going to see her when you get home?"

Dusty rubbed the back of his neck and slid off his jacket behind the seatbelt. "Can you help me? I need you to grab that."

I pulled at his empty coat sleeve and yanked. His t-shirt rode up a little in the back, and his plaid boxers poked above the waistline of his pants. Jolts of electricity traveled through me and I reminded myself to keep it together.

"Probably not. I think we've had enough of an adventure for one week. I don't know if my brain or body can handle her drama, too."

I wanted to touch him, reach out and stroke his thigh, but I couldn't. I shouldn't. We were nothing, but this sudden reminder that he was attractive to other women rubbed me in ways I hadn't allowed in years. Yet my body remembered.

"I hope it works out for you." It was a lie, but I wanted him to be happy. With me in Florida, there was no sense in entertaining the idea of us reconnecting. My sexual brain smothered my logical brain, reminding me that sex didn't equal a relationship.

"What will you do when you get home?"

"Get in my sweats, order Chinese food, and watch a movie. What about you?"

My parent's faces popped into my mind and disappointment swept over me. I wasn't ready to see them yet. "I don't know. Would you mind if I hung out with you for a few hours?" My confidence barreled out of me like a bull rider. "I wouldn't mind watching a movie with you, seeing your apartment and pieces of your life." I studied his profile and watched the corner of his mouth twitch into a smile.

"I'd love that."

"Dusty?"

"Yeah."

"I'm happy I bumped into you. I've thought about you often over the years, and it's been nice catching up." There. It was in his hands now. He had agreed to allow me to enter his home, and I hoped we could continue our friendship. I sometimes wondered what would have happened if I never went to that concert and met Trevor. Trevor was everything Dusty wasn't... moody, intense, and mysterious. His secrets pulled me toward him and kept me anchored to him until they became too heavy and nearly pulled me underwater. Looking back at my eighteen-year-old self, I needed Trevor to search for who I wanted to be as I grew from a child to an adult.

"Yeah, it's been interesting." Dusty interrupted my thoughts, and my mind returned to him. "You say you thought of me, but why didn't you ever call me? I was angry at you, but I waited for you. When freshman year ended, I realized I was in the same spot as I was when you left me, and I hated that. Why didn't you ever reach out?"

Thinking long, I responded, "Even though you told me you needed a break, I knew dating other men was wrong. We were dangling by a thread, but I was too afraid to cut the cord. After Trevor and I split, I thought about you, and I was ashamed."

"Of what?"

"My behavior. You were the best thing that had happened to me, but I thought there was something better out there. Especially in college. Weren't we told that college was when you found yourself? I couldn't do that if I was attached to you, so I pushed you away. I had never been taught how to handle conflict, and I learned that when things go wrong, I run away."

"So you ditched me, and I never heard from you again."

"Right. Well, I did call you."

"Almost a year later. The damage had already been done."

My hands shook in my lap. "I thought that if I never faced you or my feelings, I could move on. When things got tough, I ran. I ran from you, I ran to Florida away from my parents, and I pulled away from Lanna."

He gave me a side eye. "That was your roommate, right?"

"Yeah, my sidekick for all of college. And the bride this weekend. She never pushed me to be someone I wasn't, but as we grew into adults, I realized it wasn't for my benefit, but because she was so focused on what she wanted in life. Our friendship was skewed, with me following her around like a puppy dog, and I didn't see it until I moved away. So I pulled away from her. We kept in touch, but it wasn't like the friendship we had in college."

"Are you nervous about seeing her again?" Dusty's voice took on a caring vibe, and my leg stopped shaking.

"Kind of, but not really. I'm nervous that I'll feel like an outsider because I allowed us to grow so far apart. And I still feel bad, not knowing about all the family she lost during COVID. Sometimes I wonder if she invited me in the wedding because she felt like she had to. Like, she needed an even number of bridesmaids or something." My face flushed and my chest got hot. The thought had crossed my mind multiple times, but I had never said the words out loud.

"I'm sure it'll be fine," Dusty said.

"And then, with my parents, my shame grew even bigger. I realized I was better off alone, because if I never got close with anyone, I wouldn't be able to hurt them. That's why I never called, but yes, I always thought of you. On your birthday, on our old anniversary, on Christmas…your face from fifteen years ago always flashed through my mind."

Dusty sighed, his breath sucking out the air in the car. "Life is all about timing, right? I guess the timing wasn't on our side."

Tired of fighting the urge to feel him, I reached out and touched the top of his hand. "I guess we missed our chance." There was a finality to my words, and Dusty didn't question it. So many what-ifs that may have changed our story, but now it was too late.

* * *

I drove the minivan into Dusty's driveway, careful to hug the snowbank without getting stuck. His apartment was cute, with balconies hanging off every floor. Whoever lived on the first floor, or maybe the landlord, had taken care to hang a wreath on the door. Even though it was February, the wreath brought cheer amongst the drab backsplash of winter.

"Cute place. What floor are you on?"

"Third. There's an older couple on the first floor and a few college kids on the second. Everyone in the house is quiet, which is great for me. I leave around five every day to get into the city."

I shuddered at the thought of rolling out of bed before ten. Usually, I didn't get home until after midnight. Counting the till, checking the next day's schedule, and ordering last minute stock created long nights and short days. "I bet when you're driving home from work, I'm going in," I said.

"It's a boring life, but it's good." Dusty unlocked the door and led me into his spacious apartment. Despite the mundane exterior, the inside was bright and open.

"Wow, check out these plants." I pointed to the windows that lined the front room. Small pots dotted each one, with different green leaves decorating the sill. "I need to take some pointers."

Dusty dropped his keys on the coffee table and slid his muscular arms out of his coat. Seeing him in his own environment reminded me I was in his space, lucky to be included. He deserved more. "Take a seat. Make yourself at home." He motioned to the couch, and I obeyed. "Do you want a drink? Or some food?"

Hearing the word food, my stomach groaned. "I am always hungry. That would be great." I heard the fridge door open and close in the other room.

"How about some nachos?" His voice carried through the apartment, and I recalled the cooking class we shared in eleventh grade.

"Sure." I wanted to see him in action, moving around his turf with command, so I gingerly moved into the kitchen. It was rather tight, so I hugged the corner wall near the sink.

63

"Remember that time we had to make nachos for Mr. Bingsley?" I chuckled. "I think nachos was my first time cooking in the oven. My parents never let me in the kitchen growing up, which is probably why I'm a chef today."

"Yeah, didn't we fail that assignment?" A cute grin met my eyes and I couldn't help but smile back.

"Yeah, he said we lacked creativity, and no restaurant would ever hire us."

"Ha! If he could see you now," he said. A comfortable silence settled between us.

"Hey," my voice softened, "let me cook you dinner tonight. Let me show you how much I've improved." I helped myself to his fridge and scanned the contents.

"You really think you can make something? I haven't been shopping in three weeks. Anything fresh in the fridge is probably spoiled by now, and I'm a bachelor." I watched his face flush and fought the urge to kiss his lips. Instead, I dropped my eyes from his and returned to the fridge.

"I can find something. You let me work my magic." Being in the kitchen, anyone's kitchen, really, brought me to life. This was my place to shine, and I didn't know if I'd have another opportunity to feed Dusty. I wanted to pour my heart and soul into this meal, but he was right. I'd have to work my magic because it was slim pickings. "You know what? Let me surprise you. Take me to the nearest grocery store, and you have to promise not to look at what I buy. You stay in the car, and I'll run in and grab all the special ingredients."

I watched his face light up with anticipation and he leaned against the counter, sending a whiff of his cologne, soap, or deodorant into my space. My body shivered inside, and I stuck out my hand. "Is it a deal?"

He took it with a firm grip and shook. "Deal."

I knew exactly what to make for him, and I knew one bite would send him head over heels back in love with me.

Chapter Eight

Dusty told me no proteins were off the table, so I raced up and down the food aisles like a kid in a candy store. I thought about the restaurant and our Valentine's Day specials that I created through hours of trial and error. The recipes included aphrodisiac-ingredients and our advertisements promised to make the night memorable. Valentine's Day was in a few days, and I couldn't help but wonder if I would find all the ingredients I needed at the grocery store.

Oysters stood at the top of the list, but I wasn't sure if Dusty liked them. Fancy in presentation, they weren't common in diet repertoire, and I didn't want to risk turning him off by trying to turn him on.

Asparagus, on the other hand, was something I could get behind. I picked up a bundle and examined the stalks, looking for a vibrant shade of green with purple hues. I squeezed, feeling their firmness in my hand, and placed them in my cart. I grabbed a package of chocolate dipped strawberries and a can of whipped cream for dessert. Theoretically, I would have made both from scratch, but time was not on my side. My parents were expecting me at some point tonight.

A box of rice and the juiciest rib-eye I could find completed the order. My mouth salivated just thinking about dinner. As I walked to the registers, I grabbed a small bouquet and a bright red candle promising to spread the scent of romance.

When I got to the car, Dusty's phone pressed against his ear. He held up one finger, cuing me to keep quiet, so I sat in the passenger seat and pretended not to listen.

He turned his body away from me and I heard a chipmunk tone chatter through the earpiece. The words were a jumbled mess, but I could sense a hint of frustration.

"I have to go," Dusty interrupted.

More chipmunk chatter erupted.

"Fine. Sure. Whatever." The phone dropped into the middle console and he turned to me. The smile didn't hide his worry, and I wanted to ask, but knew it was none of my business.

"Who was that?" I couldn't help myself.

"Remember when I said it was complicated?"

"Yeah." I encouraged him to continue with my gentle head nod.

"Complicated just became finished."

My heart jerked toward him, seeing the hurt in his eyes, but I couldn't quite understand why. Hadn't he just told me they had an open relationship and it wasn't for him? "I'm sorry."

He put the car in reverse and backed out of the spot. We headed toward his apartment and I pushed the bag of food behind my feet. Maybe a romantic dinner wasn't the best decision. My mind quickly went into overdrive, trying to recall if I saw any other food in his house.

Focused on the road and lost in his own thoughts, I leaned my head toward the window and looked at the sky. "It's snowing." The white fluffy flakes splattered the windshield.

"Welcome to New England," Dusty muttered.

"Sorry. I was just commenting on the weather." My voice held more snark than I wanted.

He shot me an irritated look. "What?"

"Nothing, it's just that we were having a great day until you got that phone call. Why are you so upset, anyway? It's not like she's the one."

"It's the principle, Cassie. Every single person I have dated has broken up with me. It's like I sit around, waiting for something to improve, and when it doesn't, I still sit there, hopeful it'll work out. Next thing you know, I'm tossed out like trash. And it started with you. I'm upset because I strung her along and she strung me along, and she was the one to break the string. It should have been me. But I'm a glutton for punishment, too weak to be in control of my life, and carrying too much baggage to find someone worth carrying some of it with me. That's why."

"I love how you're blaming your history with women on me. Like I controlled your life over the last fifteen years." I pushed the bag further under the passenger seat with the heel of my flip-flop, feeling the stems of the roses break under the cheap rubber of my heel.

When we got to his apartment, he slammed the door shut with an extra loud clang, and the car shook. Without waiting for me, he stomped his boots on the steps leading up to the porch. I fumbled with the bag and my chocolate-covered strawberries slid out the ripped plastic, crashing onto the snowy ground. "Oh no," I yelped.

Dusty peeked over, seeing the decadent dessert smooshed into the snowbank. "What happened?" His voice carried concern instead of irritation.

I made a face as I retrieved the fruit, dropping it back into the box. "The bag must have ripped." I hid the flowers behind my back, feeling silly for putting so much effort into this dinner, and trudged over to him.

He pulled me into a hug. "I'm sorry for before," he said. "I shouldn't have acted that way toward you. I was mad and needed to get it out."

I shifted my weight from one foot to the next and handed him the flowers. "Do you want me to stay? I can go if you'd rather be alone."

"Chocolate covered strawberries and flowers? And you're asking to go? No, I have to see what Chef McCarthy can make, because you talk a big game. I love surprises, and can't wait to see what you come up with." He sniffed the flowers. "This is the nicest thing you've done for me in the past fifteen years."

My heart thudded and my stomach fluttered. I scanned his body, paying close attention to his posture. His arms hung loosely at his sides and his feet stood shoulder-width apart. The flowers hung at his hips. He reached out and took the bag from my hands.

"I promise I won't look," he said with a wink.

His intense eyes warmed me from the harsh Massachusetts cold, and his smile lit a fire within me. I knew if I left, I would never see him again, and I wasn't ready to say goodbye. I couldn't risk going back to Florida with unfinished business… even if he had unfinished business himself.

I forced the idea of another woman from my mind and followed him up the stairs.

* * *

"Mmmm," Dusty mumbled. "This is the best ribeye I've ever tasted."

I beamed at him, admiring how he cut his steak into bite-sized pieces, and then held it in his mouth for a moment before chewing. This was a man who appreciated things.

I cut the green stalk soaked in butter and lemon, and stared into his eyes while I guided the asparagus tip to my mouth. I closed my eyes when I chewed and licked the remaining butter from my lips. I didn't know if dinner was turning him on, but I was having fun trying.

"You are an amazing chef," he said.

It meant something coming from him. I'd confessed my dream of running my own restaurant back in high school, and to know that he was proud of me filled a void I didn't know existed. "Thank you."

As we ate dinner, my body responded in overdrive to all the memories that flashed before me. "You know," I said, reaching for my water, "you haven't changed a bit."

He chuckled. "I don't know if that's a good thing, but thank you."

"No, really. You're still the caring, kind man I fell in love with."

His hand stopped midway to his mouth, his fork holding a piece of steak. His eyes held mine and I stopped breathing.

"I mean, it was puppy love, but you were the first man I loved," I stuttered.

"You loved me?" His eyes glistened.

"You know I did. I was crazy about you."

"So, what exactly changed?"

I leaned forward, not sure I wanted to rehash this for the third time in three days. "I told you. College. I needed to find myself. Make mistakes, do stupid things. By the time I realized how much I had screwed up with you, you were dating someone. I think her name was Tracy."

He nodded and chewed slowly, like the sound of his jaw clenching the food could interfere with his ability to hear if he ate too quickly. "Yeah. That was sophomore year."

The only sound at the small bistro table was the clinking of silverware and plates.

My heart fell to my toes, and anguish over my stupid decisions seeped into my vision. I collected the empty plates and walked them to the kitchen sink. Tiny tears sprang from my eyes and I sniffled them away.

I sensed his presence behind me, but I didn't hear him come in. Wiping at my eyes, I turned and flashed him a smile. I wanted to say something, but the words remained stuck between the back of my throat and my brain. The hot water ran across my hands and I scrubbed the dishes clean, focusing on each movement. "I'll do the dishes and then we'll do dessert."

I felt a hand brush across my waist, and when I turned, he was there. His shaggy hair, deep-set eyes, and chiseled face were right there. He leaned down and kissed me, first gently and then harder. My mind whirled like a washing machine, desperately trying to hold on to the present. He reached behind and turned off the water, and led me to his bedroom door. His eyes held my gaze, like he wanted my permission, and I responded with a tug on his shirt, pulling him against me.

I wanted this, and I needed to know that he wanted me too. He led me to the bed, and I fell upon his soft mattress. This may be the last time I'll see him, and I needed to know if our breakup was a big mistake. Or a catalyst to figuring out what I wanted. And maybe Dusty wasn't just what I wanted, but also what I needed.

* * *

Later that night, I rolled onto my back and my heart pounded like the steady beat of a bass drum. My eyes closed and my mouth opened. I reached across and touched Dusty's bare chest. Tiny, soft hair met my fingers, and I ran my nails up and down. I hadn't seen him in decades, yet the familiarity of his chest felt like yesterday. He had stayed in my heart all these years, even though I did everything in my power to eject him from my life.

Realizing we crossed an invisible line of intimacy, my heart seized and my blood raced up and down my extremities. By being vulnerable, I had opened Pandora's box, and the emotions of lust, desire, and regret poured over me like a rainstorm in August. As long as I stood under the umbrella, it was beautiful, soothing, and comforting, but as soon as I stepped beyond the safety of the canopy, I was at risk of drowning.

A quick glance outside the window revealed darkness and reminded me that real life would begin again. I couldn't stay, but I also didn't want to see my parents. Caught in a conundrum, I debated getting a hotel.

"Dusty?" I asked, my voice barely a whisper.

"Mmm?"

I stared at his beautiful face and ran my hands up and down his jawline. He smacked his lips and my thumb tugged at the loose skin, revealing a sexiness I couldn't shake. "Was what we did bad?"

He leaned on his left arm and looked at me. His fingers ran up and down my skin, and I snuggled closer. His eyebrows knit together and then relaxed. "Why would it be bad?"

"Because you're complicated. We're complicated." I wanted to ask if we could work, but I knew the answer. Living three hours by plane was not ideal, so I accepted our moment as the closure I needed.

"What are you hoping for?"

"I don't know. Nothing." I wanted to ask him to come to Lanna's wedding with me, but it felt too personal, like the risk of rejection was too strong. I pulled my legs over the edge of the bed and wrapped the sheet around my body. "I'm leaving in a few days," I said to no one.

"We'll keep in touch." He moved beside me and kissed my lips again.

As much as I wanted to try again, I knew we wouldn't work, and his response solidified my assumption. The obstacles to a long-distance relationship and an ex-boyfriend who already had packed so much of my baggage would never work, and I couldn't risk hurting him again. My brain and heart collided and all I could do was watch.

I picked up my discarded clothes and dragged them onto my body. Everything felt weird. Like time had slowed, and I was stuck in a place where real life wasn't happening. I grabbed my flip-flops and slid my pink-coated toes into them.

"Are you leaving?" He jumped up from the bed and slid his pants over his plaid boxers.

"Yeah." Tiny tears stung my eyes. "I have to get home and see my parents."

"Just like that?" He grabbed my wrist, and I jerked it away.

"Yeah." My mouth said yes, but my head shook no. "It

was really great seeing you," I said. My voice quivered, and I swallowed the bubble growing in my throat. Heat pumped out of my chest, and my fingers trembled. "I have to go."

He watched me walk to the door but didn't follow.

"Bye, Dusty." I couldn't look at him. He was a reminder of who I should have been, and even in my lame attempt to protect him by leaving, I had hurt him again. I bit down on my lip as I slowly closed the door. Instead of walking down the stairs, I leaned against the wall and allowed the tears to fall. My legs couldn't hold me up any longer, and I slid to a squatting position, silently wailing. My heart was breaking again, even though I desperately held it together with putty hands.

Foolish that I allowed myself to open up to him again, I regretted getting in the car. If only we hadn't bumped into each other at the airport. If only Jewel hadn't flaked on me, and put it in my head that Dusty and I had chemistry. If only I hadn't left him for another guy. If only...

I sat there for who knows how long, wanting him to open the door and check on me, but he never did.

Once my bleary eyes cleared, I pulled myself up and sneaked to the minivan. I had a short drive to clear my head, put on a cheerful face, and face my parents. I had already hurt one person today. I hoped when I got home, I wouldn't recognize the same disdain on my parents' faces, too.

I texted mom, telling her I was on my way. She returned my text with a smiley face, and a sad smile creeped up my lips. Building up the armor around my fragile heart and chaotic mind, I drove to Providence, praying their tiny one-bedroom apartment wouldn't break my already fractured heart.

Chapter Nine

My parents had moved into their apartment building overlooking the Providence River during my junior year of college. At that point, I couldn't transfer to a state school to save money without having to repeat core classes. It would delay my graduation by a year, and it made little sense from a time or money perspective.

Their building towered over the buildings beside them, and when I looked out their living room window, I could see the skyline of Providence. It was rather pretty at night, and I knew my mom enjoyed watching the sunrise with the shadowed buildings dotting her view in the distance.

My great-grandparents came to America from England and Italy with the goal of forging a new life. My grandparents watched their parents struggle, and that immensely pressured my mom and dad to be financially secure. When they lost the house, both sets of grandparents likely rolled in their graves, for I had destroyed everything they fought for.

My senior year of college, I pulled away from my extended

family. I couldn't take their judgy looks, and I knew they thought I had put my happiness before my parents' needs. It was too much, so I blamed my absence on my studies. After ten years of sticking my head in the sand, my relationship with my cousins had withered to nothing.

I rode the elevator to the seventh floor and knocked on their door, like the guest that I was. My father's frame appeared in the doorway, his forehead shining in the overhead light, exaggerated by his slightly receding hairline. His hair appeared grayer since I last saw him, and he sported new glasses.

"Cassidy!" He held his arms out to receive a big hug, and I obliged. The warmth from his positive reception penetrated my timid skin. "You look wonderful."

"Thanks, Dad." I smiled brightly, despite my sour mood. "Is Mom home? I smell spaghetti sauce."

"Yeah, yeah, she's been cooking all day. We thought you'd be here earlier, so we ate without you." He escorted me into the apartment, and I saw Mom wipe her hands on her apron. The clock behind her read nine-forty-five.

"Sorry, it took longer than I expected," I said, looking around the room and avoiding my dad's eyes. The apartment looked exactly as it did the last time I visited. My high school graduation photo rested on the wall behind the television, and several plants filled the end table beside the window. The plants had grown, reminding me I hadn't been home for quite some time.

"Kitty-Kat! Are you hungry?" Mom held up a sauce-coated spoon at her exuberance. "I have meatballs."

"Yum. It smells delicious." Seeing how much effort she put into my visit, I couldn't tell her I wasn't hungry. It was nearly ten, and I should have been in bed, but I couldn't disappoint her again. I followed her into the kitchen and helped myself to a petite bowl of pasta, sauce, and one meatball.

"Garlic bread?" Dad asked.

"No thank you, this is great."

Mom and Dad watched me eat, and an uncomfortable silence settled between us. The occasional slurp of noodles escaped from my mouth, and I swiped at my chin self-consciously, thinking about Dusty and the pizza.

"How was your drive?" Dad asked.

"It was fine, but long. I'm actually exhausted. I'm looking forward to sleeping in tomorrow."

"Well, there are sheets and blankets on the edge of the couch. We'll try to be quiet in the morning." Mom nudged Dad with her elbow. "Ready for bed?"

"Yeah. Night, Kat," he said. I watched Mom and Dad exit the kitchen and disappear in their bedroom before I threw the rest of my dinner in the trash. My stomach was still tangled in knots, and I couldn't eat any more.

That night, I tossed and turned on the uncomfortable sofa. Without it being a sleep sofa, it was smaller than my college bed, and the puffy sewn cushions prevented me from lying on my back. My eyes remained closed, but my brain churned like a tornado. Regret haunted my sleep, and I spent most of the night begging my brain to surrender its constant chatter and let me fall into a dreamless state.

Mom and Dad promised to keep quiet in the morning, but that wasn't possible in their tiny shoebox. The building was rather old, so every step resulted in a creak and groan amid the floor boards. My eyes opened at seven as the scent of coffee drifted from the kitchen to the couch. I poked up like a whack-a-mole and rubbed my eyes.

"Morning," I said.

"Morning, Cassidy. Coffee?"

Dragging myself off the couch, I roamed into the kitchen and grabbed a mug. "Thanks."

"What are your plans today?" Dad asked.

"Tonight is the rehearsal in Gloucester. I'm getting a hotel at the place where the wedding is. I'll be there two nights and drive back here on Sunday. My flight leaves on Monday evening. I'll probably head out around two." Hearing myself list off the events over the next few days put me back on that hamster wheel of life. I thought life in Florida was crazy...I couldn't wait to get back to the place where the only person I had to worry about was myself. "You have my dress and stuff, right?"

Mom bit her lip and raised her eyes to the ceiling. "I know you said you were sending it, but did you? We haven't gotten anything."

Lanna's wedding blew up before my eyes, and I nodded. "You didn't? I sent it a week ago. It was a big box." I spoke slowly, like maybe if they caught every word, they would understand. I gesticulated to demonstrate the size.

"No..." Mom's voice trailed to nothing, and I leaned forward, waiting for a 'but'.

"No?"

"No. Louis, did you notice any mail slips?"

My dad scrunched his forehead. "No."

Panic erupted through me. "It was my bridesmaid dress, and my shoes, and the jewelry. I mailed it First Class. It should be here by now. The wedding is tomorrow. What am I going to do?" I guzzled my coffee, trying to wake up my brain so I could think clearer.

"Do you have the tracking number?" Mom asked.

"Yeah, in Florida." I saw the post office slip secured to my refrigerator with a magnet.

"Is there anyone you can call? Anyone with a key who can read off the number for you?"

I racked my brain, thinking who had a key to my apartment. There was the main office who had a master key, but I didn't want them going into my apartment if I wasn't home. It was too late anyway. If it was lost in the mail, I would never get it in time. Lanna was going to kill me.

"No, mom, the wedding is tomorrow!" I placed the empty cup in the sink and circled the table, stopping now and then to gaze into the river, as if it held all the answers. My fingers moved to my mouth, and I bit along the cuticles, spitting out dead skin every few seconds.

"I'm sorry. I wish I had better news for you." Dad removed his glasses and rubbed his eyes.

I moved to the couch and pulled off the blanket and sheets, folding them neatly and placing them on the corner cushion. "I gotta go." I dashed into the bathroom with my overnight bag and pulled on a pair of jeans and t-shirt. "Mom? Can I borrow a sweatshirt?"

"Where are you going?" Mom asked as I moved through the apartment, sliding on my sandals and pulling a Block Island sweatshirt over my head.

"I can't not have a bridesmaid dress. I have to go shopping, and once I find something that might work, I have to call Lanna." I felt like a crazy person grasping at straws to regain control.

"Let me come with you." Mom threw her coat over her sweater and retrieved her purse. "I'll drive." She quickly kissed Dad and pushed me out the door. "Don't worry. It'll all work out. It always does."

I appreciated the sentiment, but I knew it didn't always work out. Dusty's face and the memory of his gentle love making washed over and through me. Things never *always* worked out, and this was another reminder of how I screwed up other people's happiness just by being me.

* * *

Mom and I walked around Providence Place mall, hitting up the designer stores that carried formal attire. After four boutique stores and one anchor store, we walked away empty-handed and hopelessness settled on my bones. Even if I found a replacement, my five-foot frame would drown in the excess material. Regardless of the outcome of our day, I knew Lanna would be disappointed. The only saving grace was that she allowed each bridesmaid to pick out their style of a similar color. If I found something of a similar shade, she'd forgive me. She'd have to.

"Do you have a picture of the dress?" Mom asked.

Fumbling through my purse for my phone, I pulled up a picture off the internet. "They have that high slit and tight bodice. Kind of like a satiny material. And they're like earthtone pinks. Kind of like baby pink, but not so obnoxious."

Mom took a photo of my photo and walked up to the sales clerk. "Hi, do you have anything in this style?"

The woman led us to the far corner of the store and we entered the world of ballgowns and cocktail dresses. Mom and I gazed over the racks, bee-lining it for the floor-length dresses along the back wall. Mom pulled out a pinkish dress with an asymmetrical top. "Like this?" she asked.

I scanned the dress and placed my hand on my hip. "Yes, but

I would need that dress altered to fit, and I don't have time. If you find something similar but in a smaller size, it might work." My hopes had slowly lifted, being amongst this cloud of silk, satin, and chiffon. I remained laser-focused and went to the next rack. Separating hangers and glancing at the shape, I pulled out a neutral shade that leaned more toward beige than pink. My heart elevated as I pressed it up against my body in the mirror.

"Mom!" I called through the store. "I think I found something that might work!"

She followed me through the dressing room hallway and I made a sign of the cross before closing the door and pulling the flowy skirt over my head. The hem covered my shoes, and I stood on my tiptoes to illustrate heels. It might work.

The slit traveled up my thigh, almost to my hip bone, and I flashed my leg in the mirror. Grateful my Italian skin accepted the sun, the color contrast between the dress and my skin looked natural. Maybe even sexy.

The bodice was too large for my small breasts, but I'd rather have it be too big than too tight. The two-inch straps hung over both shoulders, and I pulled at them to see if the bodice would fall more naturally. It did.

"Can I see it?" Mom called from the other side of the door.

I opened the door and took a step out of my dressing room and into the triple mirror area down the hall. Without shoes on, the dress was a tripping hazard. I stumbled and returned to my tiptoes, slowly turning in a circle.

"It's beautiful. Do you think it will work?" Mom squinted her eyes and tipped her head, taking it in from various angles.

"Do you still sew?"

Mom's eyes widened, and she took a step back. "No, no, this

is too big a night for me to screw up. My sewing skills are rusty, at best."

"Mom, please? There's no way we'll find a seamstress who can get this done for me in twenty-four hours. You're my last hope." I ran my hands down the smooth fabric. "Besides, you didn't screw it up. I did. I should have checked days ago to make sure you got the dress. All you would do is help me fix it."

"I don't know. I don't own a sewing machine anymore, and I certainly can't do it all by hand."

Tears built behind my eyes and panic set in again. "Do you know anyone who does? Anyone who can help? What am I going to do?" I hadn't even checked the price tag, but if I could make it work, the price didn't matter. I deserved to go broke if it meant preserving Lanna's night.

"Eh...I can reach out to the community center. Maybe someone knows someone."

"All I need," I said, "is to have the straps shortened. I can buy a push-up bra to fill this out." I motioned to my chest area. "And the hem of the skirt raised an inch. That's it. But first I need to ask Lanna."

I lifted the skirt and raced back to the dressing room and grabbed my phone. "Mom, take a picture of me?" I handed her the phone and pulled the straps up slightly. I flashed my most enthusiastic smile, as if buying a bridesmaid dress the day before the wedding when you already had one, was totally acceptable.

Hi Lanna! Good news and bad news. My dress for tomorrow never made it. Will this work?

I sent the image and held my breath. I saw the three dots blinking for far too long. Finally, my phone dinged. **Does it fit?**

No, but it will. Just a few minor adjustments.

More blinking dots. My heart raced, and I held my breath. **Sure.** I knew it wasn't an enthusiastic sure, but it was this or I wasn't in her wedding.

"Okay, I guess this is it," I said to my mom. "Hopefully, someone can help us."

We moved to the shoe department, and I grabbed the tallest metallic heels I could find. Before I could back down, I handed the cashier my credit card and grabbed the garment bag. While we marched to the car, my brain ran on overdrive navigating Plan B and C. Some way or other, this dress was getting altered today.

I looked at my mother's slight frame and short stature. "Oh, I might need to borrow a dress for the rehearsal dinner. I can't afford to buy another one, and it's just one night. Do you have anything?"

Mom placed her arm across my shoulder and pulled me tight. "I'm sure we can find something."

When we got to the car, I pulled up my email and canceled my hotel reservation for the night. Without a dress, I had to come back to Providence.

Chapter Ten

꧁ᥫᩣ꧂

That evening, I kissed Mom on the cheek and grabbed my purse. "Do you think you'll be able to get it done tonight?" The short, black dress I had found in her closet swished as I hurried around their apartment, looking for my keys. It wasn't something I'd typically wear, but beggars couldn't be choosers. "Here they are." I stuffed them in my purse and threw my bag over my shoulder.

"Yes, yes. Roberta lives down the hall. She said I could use her machine." Mom smiled at me, and trepidation peeked through her pupils.

"Thank you. I know it'll look great," I said.

When we had returned from the mall, Mom put me in the bathroom with the dress and her sewing kit. As I stood between the tub and sink, Mom sat on the bathtub edge, with sharp pins in her mouth, ready to attack. She laced the pins along the bottom and the strap edges, pulling it higher and tighter. "It will be fine. Don't you worry," she had said.

Checking my watch, I kissed Mom and Dad goodbye, thankful for their understanding. "I'll be home late tonight, so don't wait up for me. I know you and Dad go to bed early, so I'll remember to be quiet."

"Have fun tonight," Dad called from the couch.

I looked at myself one last time in the mirror and raced to the car, holding my shoes in one hand. My heels flipped against the rubber soles of my flip flops.

The familiar drive toward Boston brought back several memories, mostly revolving around concerts and ball games. As the traffic flow slowed, I knew I was getting closer. Although it was toward the tail end of rush hour, traffic never stopped around the city. I peered at my GPS as it guided me into the church parking lot. I had three minutes to spare, so I swapped out my shoes.

Running into the church, I found Lanna in a short, pink cocktail dress. Love and celebration exuded from her glowing face. The skirt hugged her butt and hips, accentuating the length of her legs, and her toned thighs and arms peeked out of the fabric. Her pin straight hair hung just above her shoulders and was closer to a chestnut brown than the dirty blonde I remembered. I threw my arms around her and squealed.

"Lanna!" I sang into her ear. "I've missed you so much."

She grabbed my hand and pulled me toward a tall, thin man standing at the last pew with a small group of men. "Cassidy, this is Graham, my fiancé."

I stuck out my hand and shook firmly.

"Cassidy is an amazing chef and best friend extraordinaire," she told the men. They greeted me, and a feeling of frumpiness settled around me. I was in my sixty-year-old mother's dress and probably looked like an old hag. I gave timid hugs to break up the awkwardness growing inside me.

"Nice to meet you," I said, thankful when Lanna whisked me toward the far end of the church.

She introduced me to the rest of the bridal party, and I said hello to her parents. I hadn't seen them in years, and they looked good. Happy and healthy. When I saw them sneak a kiss in the back, I wished for the same level of connection for Lanna and Graham.

The rehearsal seemed easy enough. As long as I remembered to follow Joanna, the spunky friend from work, I wouldn't mess up the order. I kept my eyes on her, imitating her walk, as we moved down the aisle.

An hour later we walked into the bright and airy restaurant for a celebratory meal before the big day. Eight pub tables pushed together created one giant dining table. Along the back wall stood a few banquet tables covered in food. It smelled amazing, and each person received their own beer stein that read "Lou's Tavern." For such a glamourous couple, it felt hokey, and I couldn't help but wonder what tomorrow would bring.

Knowing I had an hour's drive back to Providence, I didn't drink, but did tuck the beer stein next to my purse under my seat. I had spent most of the night watching Lanna and Graham flirt and entice each other with their eyes, and my heart swooned. It was so obvious they were in love; it made my insides tug with desire, and all the ill feelings I had experienced when I first heard about Graham disappeared. I wanted that. I never thought I did, but I wanted a person who got me.

I made small talk with the surrounding people, taking in their varying levels of inebriation. Joanna always had a drink in her hand, and I couldn't help but watch her navigate the room. Her sexiness moved from her sashaying hips to her confident smile, and I noticed all the men watching her. She didn't stay with the other bridesmaids, and I wondered if she was as much of an outsider as I was.

After dinner, I checked my watch and stood to leave. I had a long drive in front of me, so I kissed Lanna on the cheek, gave Graham a hug, and said my goodbyes.

By the time I got home, it was close to midnight, and all the lights were off. I stripped out of my stretchy dress and threw on my pajamas. The cotton material nourished my skin like a warm bath. While brushing my teeth, I noticed the dress for tomorrow hanging from the shower rod. It looked beautiful and sparkled under the bright light. The alterations were impossible to see, and holding it up to my body, the edge of the skirt dragged on the floor. It was better, but it wasn't perfect. It seemed Mom had come through for me after all.

I smiled, dreaming about the fun I would have at the wedding, and tucked myself into the worn sofa. Maybe coming home wasn't the worst thing after all.

* * *

The next morning, someone rubbed my shoulders, and my eyes jolted open. Mom sat on the edge of the couch cushion with a cup of coffee in her other hand. "Wake up. Get going."

I rubbed my eyes and looked out the window. The bright blue sky shined through the sliding glass door, and a splattering of clouds decorated the buildings across the street. "What time is it?"

"Nine-thirty. Don't you have to go to the wedding?"

My brain clumsily calculated the time it would take for me to get to the hair salon. I jumped off the couch with renewed energy. "Yes. I do. I have to go."

I raced into the bathroom, showered in record speed, and brushed my teeth. Lanna had scheduled time with her bridal party at the hair salon for twelve. The wedding started at four. I threw my makeup in my bag, unsure if makeup was part of the deal, and unhooked the dress from the back of the pantry door.

I double checked my undergarments and shoes, kissed my mom and dad on the cheek, and sprinted to the door. "I'll be home tomorrow sometime. Love you, and thank you." I held up the dress and grinned. It may not be perfect, but it would have to do.

The drive up 95 was easy, with few people traveling north mid-morning. Lanna lucked out with the weather. Despite the snowy backdrop and chilly temperatures, the gorgeous blue sky reminded me of spring. It would brighten anyone's mood. I listened to music from college and pumped myself up for a fun night, filled with dancing and drinking.

Surprised by my eagerness, I took a deep breath, pulled back my shoulders, and reworked the night in my mind. Dancing, drinking, and sleeping like a baby in the hotel sheets. Pleased that I had booked a room at the place where the reception occurred, I let all my anxiety go, excited to enjoy myself.

The hair salon stood right off the highway, and I pulled into the parking lot with twenty minutes to spare. I could see Lanna and a few of her bridesmaids inside, and a sudden wash of nerves settled on me. Honored when she asked, I now felt like an outsider walking into a party already in play. I should have opened up more last night, instead of observing, but there were enough people and enough distractions. No one had noticed me sitting alone.

What if I didn't connect with her friends and the entire day was awkward? We met briefly last night, but I kept to myself. Pushing the inferior thought away, I climbed out of my car and strutted into the salon.

"Cassie!" Lanna yelled, wrapping her arms around me. "Do you want a glass of champagne?"

I did, but I shook my head no. There would be plenty of drinking later on.

She reintroduced me to her three closest friends and relatives, and I smiled and waved. Joanna was the vivacious brunette I had watched the night before, Samantha was Lanna's older sister and maid of honor, and Kendra was a friend from her sorority.

Lanna grabbed my coat and hung it on the coat rack near the door. "This is Breanna," Lanna said. "Michaela, and Trishelle." She pointed to the far end of the room. "They're doing our hair and makeup."

Breanna, with the half-shaved head, tattoos up and down her arm, and nose piercing, waved and flipped the sign to closed. "Alright, ladies, let's get started. Over here, you'll find champagne, chocolate-covered strawberries, and water."

The chocolate-covered strawberries reminded me of dinner with Dusty, and I looked away. I gulped my water and grabbed a handful of chocolate candy from the candy bowl near the register instead.

I didn't know how I wanted my hair to look, so I sat in the comfy chairs facing the stylists and watched Lanna, Kendra, and Samantha get started.

Joanna sat beside me and asked, "So how do you know Lanna?"

"She was my roommate in college."

A wide smile erupted across her face. "Cute! Lanna and I

met at work a few years ago. It's been fun helping her plan the wedding."

A pang of jealousy poked through me, so I changed the subject. "What does your dress look like?" Since Lanna gave us the freedom to pick our own as long as it stayed in a similar color hue, I had to see. Joanna pulled up a stock photo of her dress on a tall woman whose legs were probably twice as long as hers.

"Pretty, I like it." It was like a second cousin to my dress. They both had a slit, and they both had a connected top, but besides that they were on different planets. "It's very revealing." I checked out Joanna's bosom. "I bet it fits perfectly."

She giggled, and said, "It does."

I pulled my phone out and showed her the same photo I had sent Lanna. I watched her face for a reaction, or some indication that I was a fake, but whether she liked the dress or hated it, I couldn't tell.

"Oh, that's an interesting color. I didn't realize we could go so neutral."

"Yeah, it looks great against my complexion," I lied.

"It's nice. Are you bringing a date to the wedding?" she asked.

"No, I live down in Florida. I'm single, so you know, it didn't make sense to drag a friend all the way up the Eastern seaboard. How about you?"

"Yeah, my date got sick last night and I hate going to these things alone, so I asked my ex to come. We're not together, but we're still friends."

I felt my eyes bulge. "And your boyfriend doesn't mind?"

"He's not really my boyfriend...just a date. I don't do well with commitment." She shrugged her shoulders and I nodded.

"That'll be fun," I said, but in my head, I saw disaster written in giant letters. I had a feeling I could count on Joanna to provide the entertainment if I found myself sitting alone at the reception.

I scanned the girls in the salon chairs and noticed their updo's halfway finished. "Crap," I said. "I still don't know what I want."

I flipped through the up-do books, searching for a model whose hair matched my texture and length. Still undecided, my name was called, and I bounced to the salon chair.

They were the professionals, right? I trusted they knew what was best for me. "Whatever you want to do is fine with me," I said.

Chapter Eleven

I loved my hair, but my makeup was too much. The stylist had curled my hair into loose waves that cascaded down my back. She pinned the front with bobby pins, revealing my glitter coated skin. My reflection shined back at me, and I couldn't help but shudder. Magenta eyeshadow screamed from my lids, and thick, black eyeliner created a wing tip that took off five years. It was such a foreign look; I couldn't imagine what I'd look like once my dress was on too. I didn't know if the makeup would match the dress, but it certainly matched the rest of the bridal party.

We stood in our button-down shirts and blue jeans along the back wall with our arms around each other's waists. Lanna stood on one side, and Joanna stood on the other. My cheek leaned toward Lanna's shoulders, but I kept my distance to prevent the glitter from smearing all over her clothes.

"Ladies," Breanna announced. "You look amazing."

I looked at myself in the mirror, learning to love my new look. The bridal party looked like something you'd see on a fashion runway, and it was perfect for Lanna's over-the-top personality.

"Do you have a veil?" I asked her.

"More like a simple tiara with a veil attached. I couldn't stand to have my hair in my face all night or wear a heavy veil. Even if it was just for the ceremony."

I totally got it. Her chestnut brown hair was as thick as a horse's mane, and likely gave her a headache just by blow drying. "You look beautiful."

We held full glasses of champagne and cheered. The stylists snapped our pictures with a variety of cell phone cameras, and the professional photographer slinked around us, taking photos from every angle.

The warmth these women emanated pounded into me. Even though I looked unlike myself, I somehow felt beautiful.

So what if I was single? Who cares if Dusty and I are history? I vowed to have fun tonight, no matter what happened.

"Where's the hotel?" I asked Joanna.

She pointed across the street. "Right there."

A slow grin pulled up from my lips and I downed the champagne. "I guess I won't be driving after all."

We hung out at the salon until all the drinks were gone, and Lanna pulled me aside. "Hey, is everything okay?"

"Yeah, why?"

"I mean, with the dress and the shoes and the jewelry and everything."

The jewelry. I KNEW I was forgetting something! "Oh, Lanna," I moaned. "I don't have the necklace. It's still lost in the mail. It's somewhere." I dropped my eyes to my freshly painted fingernails. The light pink color sparkled under the light. "I'm sorry."

She shook her head and hooked her arm through mine, leading me to her pocketbook in the back of the shop. "Remember what they called me in college?"

"Elantra? For your car?"

"No! They called me Don't Lose It, Lanna. I was so disorganized back then. Papers shoved in my backpack, my laptop left at the library, triple booking my Friday night plans... don't you remember?"

I did, I guess. "What I remember about you was how you always wanted to be where the action was."

"Well, Graham is type A to my type B, and he is the reason this wedding has gone off without a hitch." She looked around the room and knocked on the wooden door. "Here. I may not be prepared, but he is." She handed me a small jewelry box, and I flipped the top open.

"No way! You have an extra?" I pulled the pendant out of the box and placed it over my collarbone.

"Yeah, because you can never be too prepared. At least that's what Graham says."

"Thank you so much." The silver heart sparkled as I admired myself in the mirror. Instead of feeling less than, I felt supported. "Thanks for being such a great friend. And congratulations, again."

We walked back to the group, where the other women stood around waiting for us.

"You ready?" Joanna asked.

Lanna paid the hair salon while we grabbed our jackets and walked across the parking lot to the large hotel nestled on the corner of the main drag.

I didn't know how I had missed this hotel when I pulled in. It was rather cookie cutter on the outside, but gorgeous on the inside. A giant chandelier hung over a series of plush leather couches facing a fireplace. The employees wore black pants with tight button-down shirts and cute neckties. I hadn't expected it to be so fancy, and I looked at my flip-flops with embarrassment. I didn't look like I belonged here.

We all checked in and moved to the top floor. Lanna and Graham had a honeymoon suite, which was where the girls were getting dressed. My room was three doors down, and I was happy we weren't sharing a wall. The fluffy, inviting bed called me to snuggle, but I pushed away the temptation as I called out to the other women that I was going to retrieve my luggage.

When I joined them in the honeymoon suite, they were close to being dressed. "Wow!" Beautiful, elegant women intercepted my vision. "You guys look smoking hot."

Joanna grinned and applied perfume on her wrists, breasts, and torso. I hurried into the bathroom and changed into my dress, praying the alterations were right. The bodice was a tad higher than I wanted, and the pendant hit just above my cleavage, drawing attention to my breasts spilling out over the top. The skirt itself was still too long, even with my three-inch heels, and I contemplated cutting another inch with scissors.

"Hey, Lanna? Can you come here?" I called through the closed bathroom door.

The door squeaked open and Lanna's gorgeous face stuck through the gap. "Oh!" she exclaimed. "Let me see!" There was plenty of room for us—for the entire bridal party—in that bathroom.

"Before you say a word, answer my questions. What do you think of the color?"

She tipped her head to the left. "Eh, it's a little browner than

I wanted, but it's fine."

My heart sank.

"And the style?"

"I like it. It'll be perfect with some shoes on."

I didn't want to, but I had to reveal my mistake. I slowly pulled my toe forward, and a flicker of silver, sparkly straps brightened the room. "These are my shoes. What do I do?"

Lanna cocked one hip out and placed her hand on her hip. "You can't do anything right now." An edginess crept into her voice. "Just be careful when you're walking. Don't get distracted, and think about your feet at all times." She walked out of the bathroom, leaving me with my too-long dress.

I wanted to shake my fist at the series of bad luck, which had followed me from Florida. I couldn't let my frustration taint the night, so I walked out of the bathroom with my head held high and my bust out. I could wow people with my upper half if I really tried, and maybe then they wouldn't notice my feet.

"Sexy kitten," Samantha said.

"You look beautiful, too, Samantha," I replied. I turned away from her and asked Lanna, "What time is the limo coming?"

"Twenty minutes." Her hands started shaking and the wine in her glass shook with a slight tremor. "You guys, I'm getting married! Whoo!"

The rest of us cheered.

"It's time to get in your dress," Joanna said.

The photographer flitted around and I did my best to stay out of the pictures.

Lanna looked like a princess. Her white, sequined dress fell to the floor with a soft flutter, making her look like she was walking on a cloud. I never imagined she'd look so beautiful, and yet my heart pulled in angst. I wanted what she had.

96

"Okay." Lanna shrieked again. "Here we go!"

The group of us climbed into the narrow elevator and the photographer worked her magic, taking photos of the reflection in the ceiling, closeups, and squished group shots. "These are perfect," she said, admiring her work.

The limo pulled into the church thirty minutes before the wedding, and the pastor ushered us downstairs into the children's room. The photographer had a field day, taking our photos in the tiny chairs next to miniature tables. Lanna paced the room, and it was clear her nerves were getting the best of her.

I caught her deep breathing and meditating in the corner.

"Lanna," I said. She whipped open her eyes, and I embraced her in the tightest hug I could without wrinkling her dress or mussing her hair. "You deserve this."

She nodded and blinked back the tears. "I can't be crying yet," she said, and I giggled.

Her mom and dad watched us from the across the room, and I could see pride and admiration in their eyes. A sadness swept over me, and I wondered if my parents ever dreamed of my future wedding.

The pastor escorted us upstairs to the main lobby, and we waited for our cue. Wedding music bellowed out of the organ, and I gripped my flowers with sweaty hands. My nervous body trembled for Lanna because I needed her to have a happily ever after.

First Samantha, then Kendra, Joanna, and me. I followed in Joanna's steps, careful not to step too close. My mind focused on my dress and I extended my gait to prevent my toe from stepping on the hem. I couldn't wait to borrow a pair of scissors from the kitchen at the reception and turn this floor length into a cocktail dress. At the altar, I turned and faced the crowd.

Waiting for Lanna to walk down the aisle with her father on her arm, I gazed out at the loving spectators. The church was almost full, and the ribboned bows decorating the pews looked like something in a bridal catalog.

Then the music stopped.

A hush fell over the room, and Here Comes the Bride reverberated off the cathedral ceiling. Lanna, with her beautiful, glittery gown, stepped down the aisle with confidence and poise. She knew exactly what she was doing and who she was marrying. Tears slid down my eyes at the sheer beauty of the event. As she approached the altar, the crowd turned to witness their "I Dos." Graham grabbed her hands and I could see them shaking with desire.

In the corner of my eye, I spied a guest in the second row on the left-hand side of the church and everything stopped. My stomach flipped, and my heart lurched when his eyes met mine. My smile fell and my heart pattered like a rainstorm. Frozen in place, I couldn't move. My slippery fingers couldn't hold on any longer, and my bouquet dropped to the ground.

Lanna turned and shot me a look, like, 'Get it together,' and I scurried to grab the flowers and return to an upright position. Facing ahead, I stared at the back of Joanna's head, refusing to make eye contact with anyone else.

I couldn't.

I thought this hell-week was over, but I was wrong.

* * *

The wedding moved like a blur and as soon as I saw him; my brain shut down and my body moved on auto pilot. Like watching a movie montage, a happy Lanna and Graham kissed, the crowd clapped and cheered, and we moved down the aisle. The groomsman hooked his arm through mine, and together we walked toward the chilly open doors. I stepped out of the crowd and placed myself in the corner, watching the church empty, and figuring out a way to avoid the confusion and conversation that was coming. *What was he doing here?*

With my face to the wall, I studied the artwork decorating the foyer. I browsed through brochures about the church and flipped them over in my hand, picking up words like *eternity,* and *love,* and *community.*

"Hey, Cassidy," Joanna yelled from across the room. I knew I had bridesmaid duties, so I turned my head and smiled. My face could pretend I hadn't seen a ghost, but my insides still trembled. I moved toward the bridal party, and Joanna said, "Photos in five minutes."

"I have to use the bathroom," I announced, and walked out of the room. I didn't know where he was or why he was here, but I was going to avoid him at all costs.

Dragging my feet, I used the bathroom, washed my hands, and gave myself a little pep talk. He had seen me, and a confused look of shock had ripped through his exterior. But why?

The noise in the foyer bounced off the walls and high ceiling, creating a gentle cacophony that grew into a monsoon. I saw Lanna and Graham chatting with her parents, and I slowly approached. There were too many people in this small space, and the walls closed in on me. Walking through quicksand, I forced my legs high, making my way toward the crowd.

"There you are," Joanna said, flashing her straight white teeth and bright red lips. She looked stunning in her dress, with the fabric tugging at her body in all the right places. "This is Justin," she said, turning to someone standing behind her, "the guy I was telling you about."

I didn't want to look, but I had to. Justin. Dusty. Justin. The connection in my brain tried to make sense of her words, but I remained glued to the spot, searching for an answer. Transported back to a long-lost memory, I saw Rebecca—teenage Rebecca—standing with us in their kitchen. He wouldn't give her the bag of Doritos, and she said, "Whatever, Justin." I remembered eyeing him, with so many questions in my mind.

"Justin's my real name," he'd said. "When I was little, my sister couldn't say it, so she called me Dusty. It stuck."

As I turned to face him, I stuck out my hand and pulled together whatever composure I could dig up, and smiled like we'd never met before. Like we hadn't spent the last few days together. Like we didn't have a history, or that I knew his body better than Joanna did. "Hi, nice to meet you."

He returned the smile, and a look passed between us. "What's your name again?" His soothing voice coaxed me to step into this new role.

"Cassidy. You know, I used to date a Justin, but we called him Dusty."

A nervous giggle erupted around them. "That's so funny," Joanna interrupted. "Wasn't that your nickname growing up?"

Dusty's crooked smile flashed to Joanna. "Yeah, weird coincidence."

"Small world," I said.

"So, Cassidy, where are you from?" he asked.

"Florida, but it's complicated." I dropped his hand and continued staring. He had gotten a haircut, freshly shaved his stubble, and smelled like I remembered from two nights before. "If you'll excuse me, I think it's photo time." As I walked away, my heartbeat betrayed me. My mind reeled, trying to find the positive in this turn of events, as I pictured Dusty with this vibrant beauty, threatening to hold me hostage.

Buzzing around like a mosquito, the photographer whirred around the foyer, my eyes adjusting to the bursts of light. She leaned into Lanna's ear, and Lanna clapped her hands. "Thank you, everyone, for coming! We will meet you at the reception. Enjoy the appetizers."

Dusty left with the crowd, and I paid close attention to how he didn't give Joanna a kiss, but a quick verbal goodbye. I wanted to know more about their relationship, and get a better sense of if he was off-limits, but I didn't know how to ask without seeming nosy. Every sentence started in my head and then halted, like I was towering over a cliff, ready to drop into an abyss.

"Did you meet Justin?" Lanna asked into my ear.

"Uh, yeah. Don't you remember him? From college?"

Lanna shook her head and scrunched her eyebrows.

"It was a long time ago." He looked completely different and carried a different name, and back then, I tried my hardest to keep my college life from my high school ex-boyfriend.

"You know, he's single," she said. Invisible balloons floated up around me and I wanted to grab them and have them carry me off into the clouds.

"Uh, no he's not. He's with Joanna. She told me about him earlier today."

"Trust me, they're not together. He's a nice guy and here because she doesn't want to be alone. It's all for show."

I swallowed the lump in my throat. "You know my ex that I drove up with?"

She nodded. "Yeah, Dusty?"

"That's Justin."

Lanna clapped her hand over her mouth, unable to hide her excitement. "It's fate, Cassidy. You never got over him."

As she led us to the limo, I considered her words. Fate was something I believed in for everyone else, but not for me.

"Where are we going?" I asked.

"Photos are at Diamond Lake. They decorated for Christmas, and all the white lights are still up over near the gazebo. We should get some shots with the moon behind us. It'll be pretty, I promise."

The ten of us filled the leather bench seats, and I wedged myself between two groomsmen whose names I couldn't remember. Joanna sat across from me, and I analyzed her features. She was smaller than me, her boobs were twice the size, and her thick hair cascaded down her back. She was beautiful, and I could see why Dusty was attracted to her. She was everything I wasn't.

Someone tapped me on the arm and handed me a glass of champagne. I guzzled the drink and pushed my head back, listening to the conversation in the limo.

Lanna was right. The lake was a perfect setting for evening wedding photos. The temperature had dropped, and I could see my breath, but I let the champagne run its course and keep me warm. We hiked down to the gazebo, and allowed the photographer to boss us around, telling us where to stand, what to do, and what expression to wear on our faces.

After the photographer had taken a few hundred shots, we climbed into the limo and returned to the hotel. My head swam with bubbles, and I felt good. Better than good, actually. I shut the door to the memories from the other night and put on my best acting face. If I could pretend we didn't know each other, maybe the night would end up better than I had expected.

Chapter Twelve

❦

The DJ announced the wedding party, and the crowd erupted. Lanna and Graham danced into the room to The Black Eyed Peas, and the crowd erupted in nostalgia. "Let's Get it Started" came out when I was in high school, and like everything tonight, my brain flew right to Dusty.

I settled at the round table near the head table with Joanna, Dusty, Kendra, and her date. One empty seat joined us at the table, and I knew it was for my plus-one that never transpired. To make it less awkward, I dropped my tiny purse and shoes on the seat. My feet ached, yet I had only been wearing my heels for a handful of hours. With dancing in my future, I couldn't risk blisters and pain.

Thumbing my water glass, I fell into a simple conversation with Kendra about college. We had traveled in similar circles, with Lanna being the connecting force, but I didn't know her well and we certainly didn't keep in touch after graduation. A giant speaker stood to my left, making it hard to hear. I leaned forward, trying to focus on her words, and ignore Dusty's eyes watching me.

He sat beside me, and I couldn't help but feel how close we were. My skin prickled and familiar goosebumps erupted across it. Champagne flutes sat in the center of the table, and a *ding-ding* interrupted the night. We grabbed a glass, Lanna and Graham kissed, and the crowd exploded in cheers. The sweet liquid ran down my throat and I didn't pull it away from my parched lips until it was empty.

"They look so happy," I said. The only person who heard was Dusty, and maybe the empty chair to my left.

He leaned toward me. "Yes, they do."

I twisted my body, still unsure of the relationship between him and Joanna. "So, Justin."

A sly grin welcomed me.

"How do you know the bride and groom? Lanna mentioned your name in the limo."

"Joanna is Jo from Boston," he said, "the complicated ex."

Under the table, I smacked him on the thigh. "Oh yeah? Why didn't you tell me you were going to the wedding?"

"Because I wasn't. She was bringing someone else, but her date canceled. She asked me to fill in, and, honestly, I'm done with what we had so I said yes. I thought we could move on as friends, that's all. We aren't on bad terms, so I am here as the fill-in."

The fill-in. Temporary. Passing. "And Lanna?"

"I don't know her well. We went out on some double dates for Happy Hour."

"Mmmm. Got it. Did you know she was my Lanna? From college?"

Another high-pitched ping rang through the crowd, and

Dusty leaned closer to me. "I had my suspicions, but not until last night."

Graham stood up with his best man, who gave a speech about brotherhood, friendship, and unconditional love. He raised his glass high and announced, "Cheers! Let's eat." The guests and bridal party swallowed the champagne, and the waitstaff emerged with the start of the three-course meal.

Grateful for the speaker beside me, I spent most of the dinner talking to Dusty like we'd never met before. We were playing a game, and I was all in. Joanna roamed around the room, grabbing more drinks, chatting with men at the bar, and socializing with her girlfriends. It certainly didn't appear like they were a thing. Maybe Dusty was a fill-in. A placeholder of sorts.

After dinner, and another glass of wine, Lanna and Graham moved to the dance floor for their first dance. I settled back in my chair and watched them, their bodies moving like one. I couldn't believe she was moving onto the next stage of her life. I imagined what would come next—babies, a permanent address, and maybe a dog.

"They're going to have a beautiful life," I said. I moved away from the table, my skirt dragging behind me, and stood at the perimeter of the dance floor. As soon as the music stopped, a hip hop song burst through the speakers, and my adrenaline started pumping. I felt the bass in my toes travel to my fingertips. I pulled my hair into a loose ponytail and bounded onto the dance floor.

Lanna stayed, and the other bridesmaids joined us, hopping from side to side, arms swaying through the air, and hips shaking. I decided Joanna wasn't so bad, and I grabbed her hands, dancing to the beat. As time went on, the men joined us, and we had a full-fledged dance party.

Dusty's stiff body stood on the outside of the circle, and now and then I caught his eye. He returned my smile and pumped his arm like a robot. I cracked up laughing as images of him at our high school dances flickered through my mind. Hopping toward him, I said, "I see your dance moves haven't improved. Same old Dusty."

He exaggerated his robot movements, and I danced around him in a circle, shimmying up and down and pumping my hips and butt with the beat. The drinks had me walking on air and all the questions from earlier had disappeared.

I moved away from him, hip checking Lanna and grabbing her hands. When we were in college, we hit the clubs on Thursday nights. Dancing was our thing. "I missed you!" I yelled in her ear.

Her warm smile wrapped me in an invisible hug, and she leaned into me. "I'm so glad you're here. You look beautiful."

"You know," I shouted, "I'm really sorry for not being there for you. You deserved better."

Her face crumbled for a moment and my breath caught in my throat. *Ugh, I screwed up again.*

A wide smile appeared. "It's okay Cas, I know it was complicated with you being so far away. And COVID messed up everything. I was never mad at you."

I threw my arms around her and hugged her tight. "Thank you for forgiving me."

Another song came on and a resurgence of energy flashed through me. Feeling out of control, but allowing it, I danced back to Dusty, who was moving his arms near Joanna. Joanna seductively flung her body on him, rubbing him in all areas, and my willpower to break it up propelled me forward.

Except it didn't. Mid-step, I stopped with a jolt and my hands and knees hit the ground. My face landed on a pair of brown loafers and a hush fell over the crowd. The music stopped, and I jumped up like a jack-n-the-box. "Whoooo!" I screamed, pumping my fist in the air.

"And that's how we do it," the DJ announced. "Remember, friends. Drink responsibly." The music pumped louder, and the crowd returned to what they were doing.

I slinked off the dance floor and stood beside the photo booth in the corner. Analyzing the damages, I saw a swollen knee, and a ripped dress. The hem of my dress had a violent tear up the back and the seam along the side exposed bare skin. The fabric covering my breasts had loosened, and I felt a little side boob poking through.

Tears welled behind my eyes as I considered my options. My entire body hurt and if I wasn't careful, I'd show everyone the goods.

A tender touch pushed against my forearm. "Hey, are you okay?"

Dusty's compassionate eyes and grin made my humiliation morph into giggles. "I'm good," I said. Hobbling over to the bar, I asked the bartender for a pair of scissors. He obliged, and I got to work in the room's corner beside the bathroom. Disguised by the column separating the kitchen from the bar, I cut in an upward motion. He watched me with awe, and his attention motivated me to keep going. Midway up my thigh, I moved the scissors horizontally.

"Almost done." I took the excess material and cut a long strip from the base of the skirt. Wrapping it around my torso twice, I tied it along the side. *There.* I may look ridiculous, but at least I wouldn't fall again. Handing back the scissors, I grabbed two glasses of champagne from the champagne wall and handed one to Dusty.

He took a small sip and eyed me from the top of the glass. "Should we get a picture together?" His head jerked to the photo booth.

I climbed inside and felt his thighs push against mine.

"You ready?" He pushed the green button and the countdown on the screen began.

I smiled, scrunched my face, kissed his cheek, and for the final picture he turned his head and his lips hit mine. This man kept me guessing, and a strong desire to rip off his clothes erupted through me.

Without saying a word, I grabbed his hand and pulled him onto the dance floor.

"Look at you!" Lanna eyed me up and down and her glassy eyes told me no matter what I looked like, she'd approve.

"You like?"

"Love!" She grabbed the photographer from the perimeter of the dance floor and pulled her toward me. "Take a picture of us," she said.

Lanna threw her arms around my waist and pulled me closer. We posed for the camera, me in my new dress, and Dusty staring at me with longing.

My hand grabbed his and zaps of electricity traveled through me. I led him back to our empty table to talk.

He leaned his head close to mine. "You look sexy as hell." His gravelly voice lit a fire inside me.

"Oh yeah? You look great yourself." My emotions spilled out of me like a waterfall. "I'm really glad we reconnected."

His hand moved below the table and rubbed my bare thigh. "Me too."

"Do you believe in fate?" I asked over the loud music.

"I hadn't, but maybe?"

"This entire week has been one weird coincidence. First the airport, then Jewel, then the drive, then the night we…you know…and now the wedding. You keep showing up in my life and there has to be a reason. It has to be something bigger than us." I felt the lump in my throat grow and I took a sip of water.

"I've missed you, you know."

"Are you still mad at me? From college?" My voice quivered, and I slowly raised my eyes to meet his.

"No." He didn't add more, but he had spoken with certainty.

"Do you forgive me?"

"Forgive, yes. Forget? Probably not, but that doesn't mean I don't love you. I've always loved you."

His hand rubbed up and down my thigh, slower and with more deliberate movements, and I leaned closer to him.

"Would your date be mad if you came home with me?"

His chuckle lightened the mood, and I stopped breathing. I had never been this forward with a man before, but this wasn't just any man. This was Dusty.

"I'd love that."

There were bigger, burning questions floating around my mind, but now was not the time. I'd had too much to drink, and my brain had turned to mush.

The DJ stopped the music and made an announcement. "Now, ladies and gentleman, the cake."

Dusty and I stood up and watched a three-tiered cake roll out on the dancefloor. Lanna and Graham cut perfect slices, but I saw the jokester look on her face. I recognized it from college, when she toilet papered the trees in the courtyard on Halloween.

"She's up to something," I said to Dusty.

Boom! Cake smashed into Graham's face, and white frosting coated everything but his eye sockets. A giant 'oh' formed on his mouth and Lanna leaned over and licked a strip of whipped cream off his face.

Turned on by the sexy gesture, I whispered, "You want to get out of here?"

A sneaky grin met my eyes. "What about dessert?"

"It's in my room."

I grabbed my purse and shoes and said goodbye to Lanna. She spied Dusty in the distance, who said goodbye to Joanna, and she winked. "Go get 'em, Tiger."

My feet flew to the exit, and I grabbed his hand in the hallway. Stealing kisses in the elevator, we barely made it to my room, where we enjoyed every last bite of dessert.

Chapter Thirteen

⋯⋯⋯

I slept like a baby that night, my inner voice quieted by the passion from after the wedding. Light danced through the closed, sheer shade, and Dusty sat upright beside me. He scrolled through his phone, watching video after video.

Snuggling beside him, I inhaled the remains of his cologne. He smelled so good; I wanted to lick his skin and taste him. "Good morning," I said. I covered my mouth, certain a foul odor of champagne, wine, and food lingered. "I have to brush my teeth."

Instead of answering, he leaned down and kissed me. "I do, too. Good morning."

I felt whole again, my previous regret no longer carrying me through life, like a lost survivor clinging to a life raft floating in the ocean. I didn't care that I was leaving tomorrow, or that Dusty lived an entire day away by car; I could only think about him and me in this moment.

I cleared my throat, knowing we had to talk about one more thing before I left. Okay, maybe two.

His eyes stared at me with concern. "You okay?"

"Yeah, um, I wanted to talk about the other night. I'm sorry for just leaving like that. I really like you. I love you, actually, and I didn't want to hurt you again. In my convoluted mind, it made sense to get out before it got too intense."

He stroked my hair, his nose inches from my own. "And how do you feel now?"

My eyes shot to the ceiling as I organized my thoughts. "Well, I feel...happy." I played with the curly hairs poking out of his chest and traced my finger around his nipple.

"Is it too intense for you?"

"Yeah, but I'm glad last night happened. All of it. I'm glad the entire week happened. Ever since college, I've carried you in my heart, hoping you were okay. That you were happy. Between you and my parents, I felt like everyone I touched got crapped on, even when it wasn't my intention. I ran from that, avoided getting too close."

I couldn't take my eyes away from the fire ignited in his gaze. "I'm sorry you could never forgive yourself," he said.

Scooting higher in the bed, I adjusted my hips to face him. With my bare breasts exposed, and the sheet resting over my waist, I didn't feel naked, but seen. "I meant what I said last night about fate. I think we were meant to bump into each other."

"What was fate telling us?"

"That maybe the timing wasn't right back then, but the timing might be right now. Don't you think? You're single and I'm single." His smile was so damn sexy. I stared at those full lips and wanted to kiss them, but I didn't know where his head was.

"But what about the distance?"

Fumbling with the blankets, I covered our legs. "Yeah, the

distance. I don't know. There are airplanes. And cars. And vacation. Plus, we haven't seen each other in fifteen years. Don't you think we have a lot to catch up on?"

He raised my fingers to his luscious lips and kissed each knuckle. "I could be your friend. And more."

I pulled my hand away and my face got serious. "I know you're okay with open relationships, and I would never expect you to be monogamous with me being so far away." It sounded so clinical, when I put it like that. "I mean, I expect you'd be dating now and then, but all I ask is that you're honest with me. If you find the love of your life, just tell me. Be the one to break the string."

"That whole open relationship thing?" he said. "That was Joanna's way of saying she didn't really like me, but she *liked* me." He flexed his arms playfully and kissed his biceps.

I smacked him on the stomach. "Yeah, yeah, so what you're saying is that she was only after your body? Your hot, sexy body?" I waggled my eyebrows at him.

"You know it."

"And you were only after hers," I clarified, picturing her svelte frame and perfect curves.

"No, I wanted more. One-night stands are not my thing. Even last night. I hope there is more." His voice dropped, and my toes tingled. "I had wanted Jo to be my girlfriend and thought maybe if she got to know me, she'd realize she was madly in love with me. But she never did, and I'm fine with that. She wasn't the one for me. I know that now."

We spent the next few hours eating breakfast, talking, and walking around the town, before heading back to the hotel. I didn't want to go home, but I had to get back to Florida, and back to my regular life.

Holding hands and walking down the main street, he asked, "When are you going back to your parents'?"

"Soon. My flight is tomorrow, and I think I owe it to them to have an honest conversation."

"Can I see you again?"

Staring into his eyes, I kissed his nose. "Yes, but you have to come to me. I can't take any more work off."

"How about next weekend?" His body tensed and he squeezed my hands.

"Next weekend!" Surprised at how quickly this was moving, I questioned if I was making another mistake. Was I ready to hold his heart in my hands again?

"Well, I have to work." It wasn't a no, but I couldn't imagine the cost would be worth the time.

"I don't care. I'll stay in your apartment and binge Netflix. I'll wait up for you. Even if we only spent three hours a day together, it's still three hours with you."

"Listen," I said, slowing him down. "March is a terrible month. Give me three weeks and I will work my schedule, chunking my shifts so we can spend time together. Plus, it'll save you some money by booking your flight with notice."

"Three weeks?" His puppy dog eyes reminded me of how he looked when we went out on our first date. He was such a gentleman, then, and I was pleased to see his manners and desire were still intact.

"Yes, three weeks. I think you can handle it."

I gathered my belongings, and he carried them to the minivan.

"You're quite the gentleman," I said.

"You don't know what you're missing."

A deep intensity moved me, and I couldn't believe the week had started and ended on such a roller coaster ride. "I'll call you when I get home. Wait! I don't have your number."

I handed him my phone, and he thumbed a text message. When he gave it back to me, I had a message from Stud Muffin. **Think of me when you read this. Remember, you are beautiful**, followed by three heart emojis. I pressed my lips against his and pushed the base of his head into mine. I didn't want to leave, but I had to.

He slammed the door shut and watched me pull out of the parking lot. I drove home in a daze, feeling the weight of the world lifted off my shoulders. I couldn't wait to call him late tonight when everyone was sleeping, like we did fifteen years ago. We'd stay up all night, talking about nothing, and begging the other person to hang up first. It wasn't childish, it was necessary.

* * *

Over dinner that night, Mom, Dad and I sat around the table eating lasagna.

"How was the wedding?" Dad asked.

I had already run down the evening to Mom while Dad was at work. Instead of going through the same spiel, I said, "It was amazing. Lanna looked stunning. The music was great, my hotel room was like a fancy boutique, and I met a guy."

"Oh yeah?" Dad's response was interested, but I knew he wanted to skate over the topic.

"Yeah, do you remember Dusty? From high school?"

Dad nodded. "Wasn't he the kid I almost ran over?"

Stifling a laugh, I nodded. "Yep, that's him."

"You should never have sneaked out, you know. I thought you were a burglar. How was I to know he was in the driveway?"

"What were you going to do? Defend your family against whoever was breaking in?"

"I was going to drive around the neighborhood looking for a suspicious vehicle. You should have told me it was you making that ruckus."

"And admit that I broke your rules? You're crazy. I almost got away with it."

"Yeah, and your friend almost lost his life."

I shook my head at the memory. We had done some crazy things back then.

"You like him?" he asked.

"I do."

"Good."

That was the end of the wedding conversation and we transitioned to the weather. It felt easier than I expected to sit in my parents' one-bedroom apartment, knowing all they had sacrificed.

After dinner, I helped clear the dishes, and Mom prepared Dad a drink. He settled onto the couch with Jeopardy playing in the background, and I delivered his brandy.

"Thanks," he said. "What is Toronto." He spoke the answer a millisecond before the contestant and grinned at his quick wit and breadth of knowledge.

"Good job, Dad. Maybe one day I'll be watching you." He chuckled and I ducked my head as I passed in front of the television, knowing how much he hated interruptions.

When I returned to the kitchen, Mom had moved onto handwashing the dishes.

"Mom," I asked hesitantly, "do you regret anything in your life?"

"No, why?"

"Like, this apartment. Do you regret having to foreclose on the house?" Just saying that word made the failure of their life and my responsibility toward their past that more prominent.

"I was sad, of course, but this is much better for us. We're getting old, and I can't do stairs anymore. You don't realize how much stuff you accumulate until you're forced to downsize."

"I'm sorry you had to go through that," I mumbled, happy to be distracted with drying and putting away dishes.

"My one regret is that you don't visit. I hope it's not because you feel uncomfortable here."

My mouth dried, and I ran my tongue around the front of my teeth. "I always felt like it was my fault that you ended up here. I never wanted to disappoint you or make you feel like your sacrifices were for nothing, so I threw myself into work, trying to prove myself."

"You know," Mom said, "we didn't lose the house because of you." Her piercing brown eyes struck mine.

"No?"

"No, honey. Foreclosure doesn't just happen. It's a multitude of bad money decisions that ultimately lead to your demise."

I swallowed loudly.

"Not your demise, Cassidy, but everyone in that situation. The economy, the way our parents handled money, this idea of keeping up with the Joneses, or even living the American dream. You know, credit cards became a thing in our generation. No one taught us how to manage money, especially when the money didn't exist. At least it felt like magic. It was trial and error, and your dad and I spent more than we earned. That's what it came down to. Really. It had nothing to do with you."

I felt a small tear slide down my cheek. "I was ashamed to come home because I knew how much you loved our old house. I thought you blamed me and I felt responsible for your unhappiness."

"Never." She threw the dishtowel on the counter. "And we weren't unhappy. Those things are nice, but they're just things, right? I'd rather have you here with me than a stuffy dining room table or fancy silverware."

Mom spread her arms, welcoming me into the warmth of her forgiveness. "Come here, Kitty-Kat." Her arms pulled me close to her, and she held me until the sobbing stopped. "We are so proud of you for everything. One day, if you have kids, you'll understand. We're all just doing the best we can."

I wiped at my eyes, feeling the puffiness grow. "Thanks, Mom. You don't know how much that means to me." Finally, the last hole in my heart from years of regret shrank. The everlasting love my parents had for me healed the rough edges, and I allowed the years of self-deprecation and responsibility to slip away.

"I'll visit more often, Mom, I promise."

I went into the living room and stood in front of the television.

"Hey, it's the final question," Dad complained.

I stepped to the side until the song finished and the final answers were announced. Dad cheered as his favorite contestant won the game.

"You good?" I asked.

He shut off the television. "You have my undivided attention."

I hurried, and sat next to him. "I want to apologize for all the years I've avoided coming home. It wasn't you; it was me, and I promise I will be more present. I love you guys, and I see all you've done for me. I tried to repay you, but it was in the wrong way. And I'm sorry. I promise to do better." Before he could reply, I hugged him and went back into the kitchen.

Mom sat at the table with two cups of tea. "So, the wedding was that good, huh?"

I stirred the steaming liquid and poured a dollop of sugar and a splash of milk into the cup. "Life-changing."

She looked at me with knowing eyes, and I felt my face flush. "I'd like to see him before you go."

"Eh, I don't know. My flight's tomorrow. Don't you think that's cutting it close?"

"No." When she wanted something, it happened. I had learned that decades ago. "Call him now and invite him over for brunch. Eleven tomorrow. After brunch, you will go to the airport." It sounded so simple when she broke it down.

"Okay."

"Okay?"

"Yes," I said. I grabbed my phone and ran into the bathroom, my chest thumping in my ears. The phone picked up on the second ring and I stared at my reflection. Gone were the lonely eyes and the slouched posture. In its place was a confidence I hadn't seen in years. "Dusty? Hi, what are you doing tomorrow morning?"

"Let me check my busy schedule," he joked. "Nothing."

"Are you working?"

"No, I took the day off. Last week was kind of crazy."

"My parents want to see you. And I do, too. Can you come over for breakfast?"

"Yeah, I'll bring the donuts." That was another running joke. When we were in high school, we were always late to school because we were making out in an empty house. Dusty brought donuts to the secretary, trying to get on her good side. It hadn't worked, and we both ended up with detention for too many tardies.

"That would be perfect." I gave him my parents' address, and the butterflies in my stomach swarmed.

I couldn't wait to see him again.

Chapter Fourteen

꧁ꕥ꧂

My mother's eyes lit up the room when he walked into the cramped apartment. "Welcome." She wiped her hands on her apron and guided him into the kitchen. "How have you been?" she asked.

"Good, Mrs. McCarthy. Good to see you again. Here are some donuts." Dusty winked at me and I grinned at our inside joke.

She grabbed the box and placed them on the counter.

"It smells delicious," Dusty said.

"Mom's been cooking and baking all morning. Pancakes, quiche, bacon and sausage, and hash browns. She's gone all out."

Mom slid the 9x13 baking dish in the oven. "Well, it's not every day your daughter is home, and so happy." She didn't need to say that I was happy because of Dusty, but it was clear from her ogling eyes that was what she meant.

"Happy to be here," Dusty said.

I led him into the living room and we sat on the couch with

my dad. My parents hadn't exactly splurged on furniture, but why would they? It was only them. Feeling uncomfortable sitting in a straight line facing the tv, I hurried to pull two kitchen chairs into the living room. "Here you go," I said. Now the three of us formed a triangle with the rectangular coffee table between us.

"Hello, Mr. McCarthy." Polite as always, he reached across and shook Dad's hand.

"Good to see you."

Dusty and Dad fell into a casual conversation while I helped Mom in the kitchen. There wasn't enough room for us to sit at the table and have the food on display, so she used the table as a buffet, and we sat in the living room. I balanced my plate on my lap, Dusty sat on the floor using the coffee table, and Mom and Dad drank coffee from matching mugs.

"Aren't you going to eat?" I asked. "There's so much food."

"Ah, I've been snacking while I've been cooking," Mom said. Her enthusiastic eyes watched Dusty and I take bite after bite of food.

"It's delicious," I coaxed. "You're really missing out."

"I'll have a donut." Mom jumped off the couch and returned with two chocolate glazed donuts and handed one to my dad.

Dad nibbled off the corner and then sipped his coffee. "A sugar rush is what everyone needs."

I rolled my eyes at Dusty, apologizing for my parents hovering. "Sorry," I said. "They really missed you, I guess."

After breakfast, I helped Mom clean up the dishes and then gathered my belongings. "Dusty, do you want to come with me to the airport?" There was no reason for him to come, but I wanted to maximize our time together.

"Sure." His smile warmed me. "I'd like that."

Hugging Mom and Dad one last time, I said, "Thank you for everything. I promise I'll keep in touch."

"Ah, you better." Mom waved the utensil in her hand, and I chuckled.

"You're always welcome here." Dad pushed his glasses up on his nose and then shook Dusty's hand again. "You're always welcome, too."

The drive to the airport was too short, despite how little we said. I knew it was time to say goodbye, and I wasn't ready for it. I wanted to pack him in my suitcase and stow him away in the overhead bins.

We returned the rental, and I smacked my head on my forehead. "Oh my gosh."

"What?"

"How are you going to get home?" I cracked up laughing at the absurdity of the situation. We were so lost in our sadness at saying goodbye, we lost the foresight of our decision to drive together.

"I'll get a ride to your parents. Don't worry about me."

"I'm sorry," I said.

"You think I didn't know what would happen if I got in the car with you? I knew, but I didn't want to say no."

My heart swelled at his sweetness. I needed a guy like him to compliment me, make me feel whole, and love me despite all my fractured pieces. "Thank you." My lips pushed into his and I tugged on his bottom lip.

"I'm going to miss you," he said. "Call me when you get home."

I walked through the airport doors and turned and waved. It wasn't goodbye, but see you later. He smiled back and waved frantically, blowing exaggerated kisses. I held up my hand, theatrically catching them, and pulled them toward my heart. With an enormous grin across my face, I walked through security and boarded my plane back to Florida.

On my flight, I settled next to an older woman with curly white hair. She held a book in her lap and scooted to make room for me to get situated.

"Thank you," I said brightly.

After all the passengers got ready for takeoff, the captain made his announcement. "Welcome to flight 2215, headed to Tampa. My name is Captain Justin Matthews, and I'll be taking you home. Life is looking good down there, with bright skies, warm temperatures, and a healthy dose of vitamin D. If you're ready for an adventure, you're going to the right place."

I double checked my seat belt and closed my eyes. Life was better in Florida, but life was best with Dusty. I couldn't wait to show him around my life, pulling him into all the quiet corners that he'd never seen before.

'You look happy," the woman beside me said. "I can't help but see the smile flickering behind your closed eyes."

"I am, thank you. I'm ready for a new adventure, and I found the perfect man to join me."

She placed her wrinkly hand on mine. "Never let him go again."

My eyes shot open, and I looked at her.

"Sometimes, you must believe in fate."

My heart skipped a beat, and I chose my words carefully. "I agree. My name is Cassidy," I said.

"Faith. Nice to meet you."

If I had uncertainties before, they were gone now. My heart on my sleeve, no longer hiding, I knew Dusty and I had reconnected at the right time. Maybe when I was eighteen, I wasn't ready to commit, but now, fifteen years later, I had lived enough life and through enough pain to know he was exactly what I needed. I was ready to go on the next adventure of my life with Dusty by my side.

"Faith." I looked at her with admiration. "What a beautiful name."

Epilogue: One Year Later

eep-beep-beep-beep. The sound echoed in my ears.

I threw my arm across Dusty's chest and fumbled with my phone. The sun had started its ascent and tiny glimmers of light poked through my bedroom window.

"Dusty," I whispered, "time to get up."

He stretched his long arms over his head, hitting the headboard with his knuckles. "Ouch. Every time." He pushed himself up to a seated position and watched me pull off my nightshirt and slink into the shower.

"Do you have a busy day?" I called through the small bathroom over the drum of the exhaust fan.

"A few meetings, but nothing big. How about you?"

I ran my hands through my hair, soaping up the roots with shampoo before facing the hot water and allowing the burning stream to flow to my feet. "Yeah, we have a corporate party of twenty-five tonight. Thankfully our best server is on and they've already selected the entrees. I'll be home by ten. Jonathon, the new manager we hired is closing."

Turning the water off, I wrapped a towel around my torso and exited the bathroom. Dusty sat on the bed, rubbing his forehead.

"You okay?" I asked.

"Yeah, just tired."

"Can you go back to bed for a while?"

Dusty worked for his company in Boston, but convinced them he could still be productive if he worked with clients remotely. He had a physical office in Tampa, where he did his work when things got intense.

"Nah, I gotta go into the office and make sure the team is doing what they need to do."

I leaned down, grabbed the side of his head and kissed him. My towel fell and I allowed him a quick peek before securing it under my armpits. "Don't miss me too much." I winked and returned to my closet to get dressed.

I had to be on the floor in five hours, but today was inventory day. "Hey Dusty? Do you know where my sweater went? I'm going to be spending most of my day in the freezer."

He retrieved it from the back of our door and handed it to me.

I slid it on and kissed him again. His tender lips hinted at wisdom and reservation. "Hey, are you okay?" Worried, I scrunched my eyebrows and really looked at him. He had dark bags under his eyes, and the creases around his eyes had deepened overnight.

"Yeah, I just have a lot on my mind." He followed me to the kitchen and poured me a cup of coffee. His captivating eyes held mine and I couldn't help but stare at him.

"What's going on?" The warm coffee slid down my throat, giving me the shivers.

"Nothing really. Work stuff, mostly," he said. His tall frame leaned against the counter and his lips turned upward into a grin. "I miss you," he said. "We're like two ships passing in the night."

He was right. When we agreed that he would move down here, I thought things would be less stressful than when we tried the long-distance thing. He got an apartment through his relocation package, plus we both agreed we'd take things slow. I had faith he was the one for me, but I wasn't ready to give up all my privacy without verifying that he felt the same.

"It's hard. We both have bills to pay. But we spend most nights together, don't we?" I searched his eyes for understanding.

"We do. I have a drawer here and you have a drawer at my place. Don't you think it's kind of silly to be paying two rents? When we could be saving for something else?"

His voice dropped and I felt my toes quiver.

"Something else?" I asked. My heart pattered against my white button-down shirt and black cardigan sweater. I couldn't help but notice the way he slid his thumb up and down the coffee mug or the way his shaggy hair brushed against the top of his ears.

I knew it was coming, by the way he shifted his weight from one leg to the other, and the way his hands rubbed his stubble. I mean, we were both in our thirties. Time wasn't on our side any longer, but here? In my kitchen with him in his pajamas? Was this really the best he could do when popping the question?

He pulled me to him and the heat between us intensified. I braced myself for his request.

"I think we should move in together."

"And?"

His phone beeped and he checked the message. "Work." His

gaze returned to me. "And what?"

"Um…so, you think we should move in together?" I prompted him to continue his thought.

"Yeah, I want to live with you, Cassie. I want to wake up next to you every morning."

A smile slid across my lips.

"And feel you next to me when I'm sleeping."

"I'd like that."

He kissed the top of my head. "My lease is up next month. Would you want me to move in here, or do you want to move into my place? It's newer. Or we can both move and get a new place."

My head swam with scenarios. It felt complicated but also compelling. "Can I get back to you?"

"You know what, let's get a new place. With two bedrooms."

My heart thudded in my ears. Was this it? Was this his way of saying he wanted kids? I hadn't realized how badly I wanted him to propose or how quickly I would have said yes. Suddenly everything felt right. "Yes!"

He smirked at my exuberance. "Yes to the apartment? Or yes to…"

"Yes to it all! We're not getting any younger. Yes to moving in together, yes to a two-bedroom, yes to the future. Our future."

Flustered, Dusty hurried to put his coffee cup in the sink. "Well, okay then."

I kissed him one last time and said, "I have to run but I'll try not to be too late, roomie." Chuckling at my bad joke, I pulled my purse over my shoulder and left my apartment.

That day, I floated through my responsibilities like an angel floating on cloud nine. Everything at work moved as expected. Inventory was ordered without issue, the large party left a large tip, and I was able to get out before closing since I had opened for the day.

By the time I walked into my apartment, I expected the lights to be off. Dusty didn't typically sleep over when I worked a double, but I found the apartment illuminated by candles. The gentle flicker caused shadows to dance along the wall.

Everything stood still as I took in the soft music playing in the background, the bottle of wine, and two empty plates sitting on the table.

"Hi." My breathy voice caught in my throat. "What's all this?" I asked.

"To celebrate." He grabbed my hand and helped me out of my cardigan and button-down shirt. I stood in a beige camisole, feeling sexy and confident.

"What are we celebrating?"

He handed me a wine glass and I slowly sipped, keeping my eyes on his. Too afraid that if I blinked, the moment would melt away with the wax drippings in the middle of the table, I held my breath.

"You know, I've been thinking…for a while now, and if we're moving in together…" His voice trailed and I leaned closer. "I mean, that's big, right? That's a big commitment?"

I nodded, my chin nearly touching my collarbone in quick succession. "Big. Huge. Gigantic." I widened my eyes for emphasis.

"Yeah, and we're not spring chickens anymore."

I squinted at him, not expecting this moment could be THE moment. "Hmm."

"And, I love you." His eyes shot up and held my gaze.

I grabbed his hand for encouragement to continue.

"I mean, I moved halfway across the country to be near you."

"Yeah." The clamminess from his hand transferred to mine and he pulled it away to run his fingers through his hair.

"And, um." He looked away and mumbled, "I've never been good with feelings."

Tipping my head under his, I looked inside his soul, feeling his intense gaze penetrate my heart. "What is it? Whatever you say, it's safe with me. I love you."

A nervous grin peeked behind his lips. "I, uh." He dropped to the floor and pulled out a small box from his back pocket. "Cassie, I love you and I want to spend the rest of my life with you. Will you marry me?" His smile froze and his eyes darted between mine.

I threw my arms around him, not even looking at the jewelry in the box. "Yes!" I buried my head into his neck and kissed him quickly up his neck to his cheeks, forehead, nose and lips. Throwing my head back, I laughed with glee. "Yes!"

Relief flashed over his face, and he took the ring out of the box and gently placed it on my finger. *It fits like a glove.* I watched the diamond glisten under the lights and admired the square cut stone. My breath caught in my throat and I threw my arms around him again, speechless.

I had been waiting for this moment since he packed up his bags and moved down here. Whenever he'd sleep here or I'd sleep there, I pretended we were married and wondered what life would be like. It felt electrifying, like my ordinary life was set on fire.

After all we'd been through…the break-up, the car ride, the wedding, the move, and now our engagement, everything seemed to fit together perfectly. It had been a roller coaster, and at times I wanted to get off, run away, and start over, but somehow, fate kept bringing Dusty into my life. I knew there was something about him…about us. We had been walking parallel lives for so many years, carrying around a brokenness that stopped us from becoming our best selves. With time and understanding, our hearts had mended and we found each other again.

I kissed him again, tasting wine on his lips. "I want to be your wife. I want to be connected to you for the rest of my life. You, Dusty, were meant for me, and I promise to be the best other half you've always dreamed of."

We sat silently for a few seconds, taking in the moment. It was a comfortable silence, drawing me closer to him. "You know, I knew we'd end up together," I said.

"How'd you know?"

"This might sound crazy, but a wise old lady once told me you were the one and I should never let you go again. Her name was Faith, and from that moment, I never gave up on us. I always had faith that it would happen when the timing was right."

Dusty carried me to my room that night, and as I lay in bed beside him, I thought about that airplane ride home. Life was all about timing, and Faith reminded me that some things were worth fighting for. I knew I was ready to open up my heart once again to the man who loved me. The man who had always loved me, like I had always loved him.

The End

***

This story evolved over multiple versions and years. Check out Up and Over the Mountain at https://dl.bookfunnel.com/bah9h8uj0s to see how it all began.

Acknowledgments

This story haunted me for years. It began as a short story, developed into a novel, and then I scrapped it and rewrote it as a novella. The characters names changed three times, the level of trauma dropped, and the love story emerged.

Without my husband's constant help and encouragement, this story would be shoved into the back of a drawer or pushed through the shredder.

My beta readers and critique partners made this story a million times better, providing questions, comments, and suggestions. Finding a group of supportive people to walk with you through the writing process is priceless, and I am so grateful I found my tribe. Granite Editorial, you've done it again, and I cannot thank you enough for all your suggestions and modifications.

Lastly, thank you to my readers and Superfans who have stuck with me throughout all my novels. I do it for you. — Edy.

Also by E.D. Hackett

All novels are available across all retailers or in my shop. All links can be found at https://www.linktr.ee/edhackett

The Havoc in My Head-medical fiction, family saga, and a strong protagonist

Reinventing Amara Leventis-new adult, best friend's wedding, Greek family and traditions, and a Greek bakery

A Match Made in Ireland-new adult, new found family, American in Ireland, college romance, and forced proximity

Farm Cove Bliss- single parent romance, unexpected inheritance, later in life love, and miscommunication trope

The Block Island Series-island life, friendship fiction, new found family, bed and breakfast life, and parent-child drama
  An Unfinished Story
  Hope Hanna Murphy

About the Author

E.D. Hackett is a women's fiction author who straddles romance and women's fiction. All her stories end in a happy ever after, and she believes in the magic of self-discovery and growth.

She prefers reading over watching movies, ice cream over cake, and baking over cooking. Although she lives in New England with her husband and two children, her heart resides in Ireland.

You can connect with me on:
- https://www.edhackettauthor.com
- https://www.facebook.com/edhackettwrites
- https://www.instagram.com/e.d_hackettwrites

Subscribe to my newsletter:
- https://www.linktr.ee/edhackett